Witch You Were Here

Erin Bedford

Also by Erin Bedford

<u>The Underground Series</u>
Chasing Rabbits
Chasing Cats
Chasing Princes
Chasing Shadows
Chasing Hearts
The Crimes of Alice

<u>The Mary Wiles Chronicles</u>
Marked by Hell
Bound by Hell
Deceived by Hell
Tempted by Hell

<u>Starcrossed Dragons</u>
Riding Lightning
Grinding Frost
Swallowing Fire
Pounding Earth

<u>The Crimson Fold</u>
Until Midnight
Until Dawn
Until Sunset
Until Twilight

<u>Curse of the Fairy Tales</u>
Rapunzel Untamed
Rapunzel Unveiled

<u>Her Angels</u>
Heaven's Embrace
Heaven's A Beach
Heaven's Most Wanted

<u>Academy of Witches</u>
Witching On A Star
As You Witch
Witch You Were Here
Just Witch It
Summer Witchin'

<u>**The Celestial War Chronicles**</u>
Song of Blood and Fire

<u>**House of Durand**</u>
Indebted To The Vampires
Wanted By The Vampires
Protected By The Vampires

Granting Her Wish
Vampire CEO

Witch You Were Here

Erin Bedford

Chapter 1

I PEEKED MY HEAD out of the curtains at the head of the grand staircase opening into my grandmother's ballroom. Magical instruments played a melodic tune as the ballroom swarmed with people. Everyone and their mothers had shown up for my coming out party. My grandmother really came through with the whole Mancaster prestige. Everyone who is anyone would come to a Mancaster party, no matter the scandal around the heir.

I wrung my hands in front of me, my hands hot and sweaty in my elbow length white gloves. They matched the atrocity of a dress my grandmother insisted was in style for these kinds of things. It was a long ballgown with so many ruffles that a swan must have died to make it. Thankfully, it was long enough to hide the fact that I had

7

secretly swapped out my heels for tennis shoes. The thought of my grandmother finding out brought a secret little smile to my face.

"What's that face about?" Dale whispered in my ear, grabbing my hand and turning me in a spin.

I giggled and pressed my hand to the front of his suit. "Wouldn't you like to know?" I murmured, pressing up on my toes to press my lips to his in a chaste kiss.

"I know I would."

Pulling slightly away from Dale's mouth, I glanced over at Ian who looked just the right amount of debonair to go with his bad boy persona. Before I could say Bob's your uncle, I was whipped out of Dale's arms and into Ian's. He didn't bother with propriety but engulfed my mouth like he was dying of thirst, and I had the only elixir to quench it inside my mouth.

A throat cleared, and I pushed myself away from Ian with a more than heated grin. Aidan stood tall behind Ian, a warning look on his face. What he was warning me about, I didn't know, but it wasn't good for a seer to have any kind of expression that meant trouble.

"How could you do this to me, Max?" A low rumbling growl came with the outraged question. I spun around to find Paul dressed to the nines and a more than feral look on his face.

"What did I do?" My voice came out trembling and breathless, far less secure in myself than I had ever been before.

"I thought we meant something," Paul snarled, jerking his hand toward the others. "But here you are, not long after we made love, still spreading your legs for anyone who will have you."

Okay, now I was mad.

Before I could let out all my rage on Paul, the curtains that separated us from the ballroom and the hundreds of guests my grandmother invited opened. Silence, pure silence. I slowly turned around to see the whole room staring up at us. Then the laughing started. Fingers pointed at us, and people were covering their children's eyes, averting them away from us.

I looked around, trying to figure out what exactly it was they were laughing at but couldn't find it. Everyone's clothes were on. No one was in their underwear.

"Dear god, child." My grandmother appeared out of nowhere, grabbing me by the arm. "At least pretend you're a real witch and cover up that atrocious nose."

"Nose?"

"Don't listen to her." Dale wrapped an arm around my shoulders. "I think it's a great nose. Really brings out your eyes."

Not at all comforted by Dale's words, my eyes shot to the middle of my face. My nose had grown three inches and turned frog green with warts and all.

The scream I let out could wake the dead and, in this case, me. I shot up out of my bed quickly and right into someone else's head.

"Fuck!" my victim and I both cried out at once. I rubbed my forehead and blinked my eyes, forcing myself to wake up.

Pale yellow walls stared back at me. Trina's mess of a desk sat on the other side of the room as well as her unmade bed, and the bed I was laying in was most certainly my own. I was not my grandmother's ballroom which I also didn't even know if she had.

"You know, I always dreamed of making you scream out obscenities in bed, but I didn't dream it involved so much pain." Dale grimaced, pulling his glasses off his face to clean them with his shirt before putting them back on.

"Sorry," I winced, smoothing the covers around my hips. "Bad dream."

"Sounds like it." Dale chuckled, reached a hand out, and placed it on top of mine, rubbing his fingers along the top. "Want to tell me about it?"

"Not really." I squeezed his hands and then added, "Just tell me, does my nose look normal to you?" I wrinkled it and turned my head this way and that as Dale scrutinized my face like a good boyfriend would.

"Besides being a bit red, it looks perfectly cute as usual." He gave me a full toothy grin that, with his shaggy reddish-brown hair, made him look more mischievous than the boy next door. Add that to his intellect and those delicious abs hiding underneath his button-down shirt and pocket protectors, and you had a recipe for one stimulating guy.

"You're so sweet, I could eat you up." I leaned forward, my hand sneaking into his hair to pull his lips down to mine. My tongue snaked out to wrap around his as I urged him to lay down with me. When he resisted, I frowned against his lips.

Pulling away from me, Dale chuckled darkly. "While I would love nothing more than to soothe away whatever has you stressed, I have to get to class. Finals, you know."

I groaned and collapsed onto the bed, pulling the covers up and over my head. "Don't remind me."

Laughing at my antics, I felt the bed shift signaling Dale's standing up. "I take it you're not ready?"

I pouted and slowly lowered the blanket. "I spent a week or so planning my booth for the fair and making my potion for class. Then I ended up in the infirmary for the weekend because I quite literally burnt myself out. Tell me when I had time to study for anything else?" I ran a hand through my blonde hair which no doubt looked like the worst case of bed head in the history of bed heads. I mean, the Bride of Frankenstein had better hair than me right now.

"Well, if you paid enough attention in class, you shouldn't need to study right?" Dale crossed his delicious biceps over each other and clucked his tongue at me. Who said you couldn't be smart and buff?

"Well, I don't know. I might need a study buddy." I batted my eyelashes at him, suddenly more interested in getting him back into the bed than whether I was prepared for taking tests.

Dale snorted and dropped his arms. Leaning over me but not falling for my charms, he pressed his lips to mine in a quick kiss. "How about you pass all your tests and I'll make you scream for real?"

Trailing my fingers along his jawline, I shivered. "And if I don't?"

Smirking, Dale crept a hand beneath my covers, placing it on the inside of my thigh. "I'll still make you scream, but you'll have to work for it a little."

His hand inched up the inside of my pajama shorts and traced the line of my panties before he withdrew it. Laughing at my pout, he kissed the top of my head and started for the door.

"Tease," I called after him which only made him laugh more. Collapsing back onto my bed, I closed my eyes briefly. I tried to think of other things than having Dale's long fingers touching my skin, his mischievous mouth kissing me, or what exactly he meant by making me scream.

Okay, that was not working. Think of something else.

School. My mom. My grandmother. Yes, that's it. I could already feel the hormones in my blood killing themselves off at the very thought of her.

It really was no surprise why I was having bad dreams. I was stressed beyond my limits. Not only because of the recent financial crisis that almost got me kicked out of school which I thankfully took care of but also because of my grandmother breathing down my neck. You'd think the only thing that was bogging me down was finals, but I could only wish finals lasted through the summer and kept me from my impending doom.

This time last year, I was planning my dorm room color scheme with my best friend, Callie. That was until my world turned upside down and I found out I was a witch. Of course, I couldn't just be any witch. I had to come from a long line of high-society Mancasters, and my mother was the black sheep in the family who dared to marry a human.

You'd think I would get a pass for not knowing who they were for the last 18 years but no. My grandmother, Mrs. Mancaster, expected me to be a right and proper witch, one of the high society and pinkie finger lifting variety. Well, I had to say too damn bad. I might have traded my soul to the she-devil, but if she thought I was going to roll over and let her run my life from now on, she had another thing coming.

Starting with the coming out party.

Jumping out of bed, I went through the motions of putting my clothes on, a pleated blue skirt and a white V-neck top, matched with the very tennis shoes I had secretly worn in my dream. After I was presentable, I worked on taming my rat nest of hair. Thankfully, my roommate and quickly becoming best friend, Trina had already left for the day. Her bad habit of waking at dawn to go for a run, something that would break our friendship if she ever asked me to come, allowed me to create my own morning routine.

Now, by routine, I meant that I usually hit snooze five times, jump out of bed because I was late, and then put on whatever clothes I had closest before high tailing it to class. However, today, I could take my time. Dale's wake-up call or rather my dream had put me at just shy of seven o'clock, and I still had until nine to get to class.

I didn't have to wonder how he got into my room. I'd given him a key recently, to all the guys actually, in light of my recent knockout. They took turns checking up on me to make sure I didn't fall into a coma I'd never wake up from. Almost like Snow White but without the evil queen with an apple. Well, maybe Sabrina would be the evil queen, but I sure as hell wouldn't ever eat anything she offered me.

I didn't bother grabbing my books because today was finals, and the only thing I would need was me and whatever was left of my working brain. I headed out of my dorm room and toward the cafeteria.

I pulled my phone out and started typing in ideas, entertaining myself on the way to lunch. Snow White and her four wizards. Hmm. Witchy White and her four wizards? Surely someone has made this story before? A quick internet search had me on an embarrassing porn site that I quickly closed, my face as red as a beet.

I stopped before the cafeteria, waving a hand at my face. I so was not going in there all worked up like this. When I trusted my face to cooperate, I entered the cafeteria.

Glancing around, I noticed I wasn't the only one getting an early start on the day. The line that I usually never got a chance to see but heard at lengths about from Trina and friends wasn't practically nonexistent, as the majority of the students had already gotten through and were already eating.

I grabbed a yogurt and a juice before paying the half-awake lady behind the counter. Turning back to the room, I searched for somewhere to sit. I didn't have to search long before I noticed an arm waving me down like an inflatable tube guy. Following the arm down to the person, I was surprised to see it was Monica waving at me.

Confused but not going to turn down an open seat, I headed toward her table. Sitting down, I gave Monica and Libby sitting beside her a hesitant smile. "What, no Sabrina today? Did they call her back to the mothership finally?"

Monica flipped her bouncy brown hair over her shoulder and laughed. Glancing over at Libby, she said, "She's funny, isn't she funny, Libby?"

Libby gave me a wide-eyed look, smiling politely, and then shook her head. "No, I don't get it."

"She means aliens," Monica tried to explain. "Sabrina is an alien who got called to her spaceship."

"Oh." Libby nodded her head like she had known all along before going back to the orange on her plate.

I wanted to like Libby for Trina's sake, but the girl was as smart as a box of rocks. I hoped all that Trina said about her was true and she was getting more out of the blonde than her big breasts. Though, in perspective, that was probably a good enough reason to date her too.

"So..." I clicked my teeth, dipping my spoon in and out of my yogurt cup. "What's going on?"

Monica beamed at me like I had just asked her if she wanted a cookie. "So, I heard a certain someone is having a coming out party."

My shoulders slumped. "Oh. Yeah." I waved a hand in the air. "You know, that's something my grandmother really wants to do."

"And you should!" Monica interrupted, reaching a hand over to touch my arm. "Having a coming out party shows you are trying to fit in with our world, not just biding your time to jump back in with the humans."

My brows furrowed. "What's that supposed to mean?"

Monica's smile slipped, and the sympathetic one she gave me was not encouraging. "Well, some people, not me—"

"Or me." Libby piped in. I didn't even realize she had been listening.

"... have been saying that you're just looking to make it so that your human friends can come and go as they please. Not that I care, humans are just great and everything, but some folks think you care more about humans than your own people."

Monica glanced to Libby and then back to me, a bit of distress in her eyes. "Keeping your dad's last name and refusing to use your legacy? That's a downright insult to the magical community, don't you think, Libby?"

Libby bobbed her head. "So not cool."

"Oh, well." I pinched my lips into a smile. "While I appreciate your concern, I'm not just a witch but a human as well. I can't just ignore one side and focus completely on the other. I did give up Brown to go to this school, didn't I?"

If anything, the smile Monica gave me before ratcheted up a notch. "Oh, of course. I know what you mean. I just wanted to let you know in case anyone decides you're not Mancaster enough to come to your coming out party. I mean, wouldn't that just be the most embarrassing thing?" She placed a hand to her chest and laughed, bumping Libby's arm when she didn't join in right away.

"Well, thank you for the heads up," - I stood and picked up my still full yogurt and juice - "but I have finals to get ready for. I'll see you later."

"Bye," Libby called out followed by Monica's sardonic, "Talk to you later!"

It was no wonder I had bad dreams.

Chapter 2

I WISHED ALL MY classes would have their finals on the same day. That way I could just get them all over with at once, rather than going to a few today and then sweating through the night over the others. Thankfully, one of the classes I had to face today was Etiquette of Magic, which had become one of my favorite classes.

"Unlike, your other classes, this semester's final will be a debate." Professor Morison announced, and the entirety of the class groaned in unison. "I know, speaking to each other is the last thing you want to do, but Etiquette of Magic is exactly that. About how you represent yourself to others magically and organically."

When Professor Morison's droning, robotic voice only earned him more huffs of annoyance, he continued as if he hadn't heard them. "Now, class, I want you to think of this not as something you have to do for a grade but as a test of what you might have to face in real life." A small smile came to my lips as I watched him effectively destroy any interest any of the female body had for him and put half the class to sleep.

I raised my hand but then spoke before he could call on me. "But what if we don't expect to have to do any of this in real life?"

Cocking a brow at my challenge, Professor Morison crossed his fingers over his chest, his eyes zeroed in on me. "Are you saying, Miss Norman, that you will not be participating in the magical community after you graduate?"

Touché.

"No." I shook my head as all eyes in the room focus on me. "But what if, for example, I decided to spend the majority of my life among humans? None of them would care if I put a spell on my doorstep to remove all dirt before entering my home, nor would they notice. If they did, they'd completely freak out, and then we have a whole exposure issue to deal with."

"That is an excellent question." Professor Morison smirked slightly but then quickly smoothed his expression over when the rest of the class turned his way. Couldn't let on that he actually had feelings, now could he? "Does anyone have a counter for Miss Norman?"

A girl in the front of the class raised her hand, and we all turned our attention toward her. "You say that applying magical etiquette in your home would only cause alarm to the humans, but my question is why care about them at all? From where I see it, they are Neanderthals who refuse to stop the cycle of violence and hatred they are in. I say let them all kill themselves off and leave the rest of us alone."

A few of the other students chimed in with hear-hears, but I only gaped. Did all the other students at Winchester Academy feel like that? No wonder my booth got vandalized. They didn't want to change. They sincerely thought that humans were lesser beings.

I opened my mouth and almost let the nasty thoughts in my head pour out but then caught myself. Clearing my throat, I glanced at Professor Morison who gave me an encouraging wink.

"Well for starters," I began in a more diplomatic tone, "I am half human. It would be obvious why I would want to spend time with those you call Neanderthals, who, by the way, have just as much good as the magical community has bad." There was a collective gasp, but I pushed through it. "Secondly, to simply dismiss an entire species because they don't do things the way that you do is not only simple-minded but downright hazardous."

"Why?" another student - I believe his name was Kyle - asked, his face scrunched in confusion. "What's hazardous about wanting to remove a whole unneeded species?"

Thinking quick on my feet, I tried not to feel like the whole room was ganging up on me. "You eat out, don't you? Go shopping? See movies? Have a cell phone?"

"Yes?" Kyle answered, not quite sure of his answer.

I could see Professor Morison out of the corner of my eye smiling behind his hand, having already figured out where I was going.

To Kyle, I said, "So what would you do if one day all those were gone?" I scanned the room with my eyes. "You can no longer call or message each other because electricity doesn't exist. There's no television because there's no one to make the shows. The fast foods you so love to eat? Gone." I snapped my fingers. "You're only able to eat what you make yourselves, either by magic or with your hands."

The profoundness of my words swept over the room. Slowly, a few of those that had been agreeing with the first girl to get rid of humanity started to frown, and for some, a light bulb went off. After a minute or two, even the first girl's lips rounded into an o shape, her brows shooting up to her hairline.

A slow clap began, and my eyes jerked to Professor Morison. His eyes locked with mine as he continued to clap, pride shining in his eyes. "And that, ladies and gentlemen, is the basis of Etiquette. Thinking of how your actions, no matter how small cause a ripple effect through others. Knowing to put away the magic carpet, so to speak, and take it out again could save your very life and that of your community."

The other students mulled over his words as if really thinking about what we had said, what I had said. It was one of the first times I had ever truly made a difference in my life. Sure, I'd made a big speech during the Spring Festival, but that was more for the judges who were grown and already set in their ways. Making them shift the way we handled human-born witches and wizards was a lot easier than changing the minds of a bunch of first-year college students.

Professor Morison had the class go over a few more etiquette scenarios before he dismissed the class. It turned out that our discussion was the debate he wanted, so we all passed our final. Not that it was that hard. Really, it seemed that as long as you were actively putting forth an effort, you could get an A.

"You were bloody glorious today," Professor Morison murmured, allowing the monotone voice he used in class to drop and his British accent to flow.

Most of the class had already bolted, happy to have finished one final and dreading going to the next. Morison leaned a hip against my desk, his long fingers tapping the surface.

"Happy to oblige." I ducked my head slightly, a faint blush marring my cheeks. I didn't know why hearing his accent affected me so. I guess that was why he hid it. However, it did make me happy to know we had a little secret between us, no matter how small.

"You know, a little birdie told me you are having a coming out party this summer." He arched a brow his lips quirked in amusement. "I didn't see you as the type to do something so... outdated."

I lifted a shoulder and dropped it. "My grandmother really wants to throw me one, and she kind of helped me out, so the least I can do is give her a chance to show me off to her friends."

"And announce you as the heir to the Mancaster name."

My head jerked up so fast I gave myself whiplash. "Whoda whata?"

Morison threw his head back and laughed, the sound of it rushing through me and settled low between my thighs. What the heck? You'd think four guys were enough for my hormones but apparently not.

"It's not that funny," I pouted, crossing my arms over my chest. "I don't know all this crap, and everyone just assumes I do."

"My apologies." He wiped a finger beneath his eyes and smiled a knee-weakening grin. "However, I do feel your distress." He tucked his hands into his pockets, his head nodding. "I too was sideswiped by the magical community when I found out about my heritage."

"Hold up." I held a hand up between us. "You were human raised?" I glanced him over, my eyes lingering on his bow-shaped mouth a bit too long.

"I know I don't look it, do I?" He chuckled lightly and shook his head, his brown hair falling slightly into his face.

I flushed. "I didn't mean it like that."

"I know, I'm just teasing." His eyes crinkled at the sides as he smiled at me. "You looked so serious about it. In any case, about the coming out party, I think it's a good thing to hold on to your heritage. You never know when it might help you out of a sticky situation."

Didn't I know it? However, it seemed to get me into more bad ones than good. I barely won the scholarship for next year because of my Mancaster heritage.

Not sure what else to say, I shuffled toward the door. "Well, I better get to my next class. It was nice having you as a teacher."

Morison lifted a hand. "I'll see you at your coming out party. If I get an invitation, that is."

The teasing tone of his voice made me blush brightly. "Oh, yeah. Sure. I'll be sure to add you to the list."

"Good. Good luck with the rest of your finals."

"Thanks." I nodded and left the room. I hadn't even started the guest list for the coming out party, but I was sure my grandmother already had one a mile long of who she thought should come. I'd have to make sure she let me put some of my own choices in there. I wasn't going to be stuck at a party featuring me where all its guests were Sabrina clones.

My next final was Potions, the one I had been dreading since I mixed the Guardian Light potion with Paul's help. The thought of Paul caused a warm feeling to settle in my stomach and not just from arousal. He'd been the first guy I'd ever slept with besides my douche bag ex, Jaron. I'd thought it would be awkward, but it was actually pretty romantic, even if it was in the Potions lab.

While the highlight of that night had been Paul, the potion was supposed to be some great accomplishment as well. The ingredients in the real world would have been tricky to get, but since Professor Bromwick had a well-stocked supply room, I got to skip that part. Brewing the potion hadn't really been that much of a challenge, just nerve-wracking. However, the hard part was the finish. Activating the potion could go two ways. One way would give me this tiny little light that would follow me around and warn me of impending danger. The other way... well, it could very well blow up in my face... literally.

The hallways were empty on my way to class which meant I was late. I hoped Professor Bromwick would even let me finish my project. I knew most teachers were pretty strict about attendance. At least they were in high school. In college, they seemed to be a bit more lenient, but I didn't want to chance it. I shouldn't have stayed back to talk to Morison, but I couldn't force myself to regret it.

"Ah, how good of you to join us, Ms. Mancaster," Professor Bromwick announced as I opened the door to the classroom. I had been trying to be quiet, but apparently, the woman had eyes in the back of her head.

"Sorry, girl problems." I ducked my head and darted for mine and Trina's table, ignoring the giggles coming from Sabrina and Monica in the back of the room. At least someone found my fake period hilarious.

"Professor Bromwick," Sabrina lifted her hand, calling attention to herself. "I don't think it's fair to the rest of us who were on time to let Maxine complete her assignment. I mean, I have my period, and I still was able to make it to class on time."

I brimmed with anger at Sabrina's words. Why couldn't she just leave well enough alone? I guess it was because she was a stuck-up bully. Even though I'd been brave enough, or maybe stupid enough, to bring her down a peg or three, it apparently wasn't enough.

Thankfully, Professor Bromwick didn't share Sabrina's sentiment. "Thank you, Ms. Craftsman, for your opinion, but I do not deduct for tardiness. However, I will ask that Ms. Mancaster be the first to complete her assignment."

Oh, joy.

Trina patted my arm in solidarity with a grim smile. I tossed her a grateful look before sliding off the stool and heading to the front. The majority of potions required activation because the combination of the ingredients alone wasn't enough to make the potion truly magical. I mean, they were just chemicals. They couldn't bring you luck or cause boils. Okay, so maybe one of those potions might be able to do that on its own with the right lethal combination. However, without magic, nothing was going to make that yellowish white substance in my bottle turn into a floating Spidey sense.

Professor Bromwick held up said bottle and held it out toward me. I took the bottle with a shaky hand, telling my nerves to knock it off before it made me drop the thing. I could feel the whole room's eyes burrow into me as they stared intently. Some of them were no doubt hoping that I got it right because they wanted to see what a Guardian

Light was, but some, namely Sabrina, were rooting for me to fail.

I held the bottle in my hand, staring down at the swirling liquid inside. I knew what I had to do. I'd read up on it extensively, but for the life of me, I couldn't get the words out. Most of the magic I'd dealt with up until this point had been just focusing on the intended outcome and make it happen with the power inside of me. However, the harder spells like the ones that paused time or made this light thing were more complicated. They required more direction.

"Ms. Mancaster?" Bromwick raised a thin dark brow at me. "Is there a problem?"

I chuckled nervously, licking my lips. "No, just working my way up to it. I'd rather not get blown up." The room laughed with me, but they were just as nervous as me.

"And we appreciate that." Bromwick clicked her tongue and laced her hands before her. "However, we do have a time limit for this class and many others to go through. So, if you would...?"

"Right." I nodded and then turned my head back to the bottle. I swallowed hard. I could do this. I rewound time. I saved a woman's life. I could make a little potion turn into a floating light. My very own Tinkerbelle.

Taking a deep breath, I focused my eyes on the concoction inside. The words didn't really matter, it was more the power behind them. The words just helped guide the magic into doing your bidding. The most powerful of them didn't need words at all. However, I wasn't about to test my limits with something so volatile in my hands.

"Come forth." The words burned coming out of my mouth as the magic pushed forward. The room quieted as we all waited with bated breath to see if I would fail. The magic of the words touched the outside of the bottle, and the contents inside moved even more rapidly than before, the part my skin touched warming. I forced my hands to hold on to it because dropping it now would be a bad idea, even if the mixture was going crazy.

A gasp from somewhere in the room filled the silence, and someone shouted, "It's gonna blow!"

My head started to jerk to the side to see who said that but Bromwick's voice stopped me. "Don't lose concentration."

My eyes squinted, and sweat dripped down my face. The chances of me dropping it became higher as my hands turned slippery. Holding my breath, I gritted my teeth commanding the magic to do what I willed.

Someone screamed as the glass container broke in my hands. I squeezed my eyes shut and prepared myself for the inevitable pain of the glass cutting into me, but it didn't happen. I opened one eye to see the glass frozen in the air, Professor Bromwick's hands up in front of her manipulating them into the trash can. The liquid in the containers, however, stayed in the air before me where my hands still sat cupped. It twisted this way and that before forming a ball that looked to be made out of rubber. Then, to my surprise and likely everyone else's, the rubbery look began to fade, and the solidity of the liquid began to dissipate, leaving a gassy substance that glittered in the light.

The strange sphere hovered for a moment and then lowered into my hands, I flinched and almost jerked away, but Professor Bromwick caught my wrist keeping me in place.

"Don't." Her words were sharp, but her eyes were on the thing in my hands. "It needs to familiarize itself with you."

Against my better judgment, I let the little ball rub all over my hands. It kind of tickled, to be honest, not at all what I was expecting. After a moment, it floated off my hands and zipped around the room. My eyes followed it, watching much to my chagrin as people lifted their heads from beneath their desks. Really, no faith at all. Once it had a feel for the room, it flew back toward me. I ducked slightly, but it didn't hit me. It stopped just shy of my head and hovered there.

"You may name your Guardian Light, if you like," Professor Bromwick told me with a small smile. I returned that smile, but she had already turned to the class. "Now, class, I recommend you all take note of what Ms. Mancaster did and how to make sure you do not make the same mistakes. To have a Guardian Light is a mark of a true witch or wizard. You should all hope to achieve such a feat."

The room erupted into cheers as I walked back to my desk. Even Sabrina clapped for me though she rolled her eyes while doing it. Whatever. I counted it as a win.

Trina shifted closer to me as I took my seat. The next person was already walking up to the front after being called by Bromwick. "So, what are you going to call it?" Trina asked, her eyes scrutinizing the small light with excitement. "How about Beowulf?"

I cocked a brow at her.

"What?" She shrugged. "It's a perfectly nice name."

Resisting the urge to roll my eyes, I glanced up at my Guardian Light. "If you're a werewolf, sure. However, I was thinking something a bit airier? I mean, it's barely even there. A name like Beowulf would be too heavy for her."

"How do you know it's a her?"

I lifted a shoulder. "I don't know. I doubt it's either, but it's easier to refer to it that way. Besides, I'd rather think of it as a female stalking me rather than a male."

Trina giggled.

"Ladies." Professor Bromwick warned us from the front of the class.

We ducked our heads in apology and lowered our voices.

"Definitely a female," Trina whispered. "You have plenty of males as it is."

"Don't I know it." I smirked at her and then went back to my new companion. "I'm thinking... maybe... something like Aris?"

"Hmm. That's a pretty name. Sounds familiar. Is it from a movie or something?" Trina tapped her chin and thought.

"No, it makes me think of otherworldly things, like a world of dragons and fairies or something. Don't you think?"

"I could see that." Trina nodded. "Alright, Aris, it is."

Chapter 3

AFTER POTIONS, I HAD time to grab lunch before my last final of the day. Aris bopped away next to my head.

What kind of warnings would it give me? Like if my period was going to come or if grave danger was coming? I snickered to myself.

My phone buzzed as I stepped into line and grabbed a tray.

Callie: Did you blow anything up?

Rolling my eyes at her text, I grabbed a plate of fries and put it on my tray before typing back. *No, and thanks for the confidence booster.*

Callie: What are friends for but to expect you to mess up? Then be there to fix it. I'd still love you if you lost your eyebrows or a nose. You didn't lose your nose, did you? Cause I was kidding about that part.

I couldn't help myself. I busted out laughing, bumping into the person behind me. "Oops, sorry." I glanced over my shoulder and then my grin widened. "Aidan, hey."

"Hello." He nodded and indicated the line had moved.

I shifted further up in line, shoving my phone back in my pocket. When I passed the next section, I grabbed an apple and a stick of cheese. "Why didn't you tell me you were behind me?" I gave Aris an annoyed look. So much for the warning system.

"I did not want to disturb you." Aidan filled his own tray with way more food than I could ever imagine eating. Then again, Aidan was built like a linebacker and probably needed all the calories he could get. When he turned his bright blue eyes back to me, I felt a warm tingle go down my spine. This guy had seen me naked. Not only that but he had helped Ian get me off, and it made me feel nervous and excited at the same time to be near him.

"When has that ever stopped you before?" I cocked a brow at him. Aidan didn't answer like I expected, and I stopped at the end of the line to pay. The cashier looked at my tray and then at my head, her eyes widening.

"What's that?" she pointed a finger at me.

I glanced around my head confused and then remembered that the ball of light stalking me to no end was of my own creation. I lifted a finger and giggled, "Oh this. It's my guardian light. Aris."

"Does it eat?" she seemed far too interested in the ball.

"Hmm." I stared up at it curiously. "That's a good question. No idea."

"Well, I better not see it picking off your plate or I'll have to charge extra."

I gaped at the woman before clamping my mouth shut and paying her. Leaving the line, I headed toward an empty table but paused, remembering Aidan.

I glanced over my shoulder, expecting him to follow me. Aidan stood there for a moment as if a fish out of the water, not sure what to do. I jerked my head toward the tables. "Come on."

Thankfully, he didn't need much more persuasion than that and followed me. Sitting down, I grabbed the ketchup bottle from the middle of the table. I fought with the lid for a moment until a large hand reached over and took it from me. My eyes watched Aidan's hands as he easily twisted the cap off and handed the bottle back to me.

"Thanks." I beamed at him, pouring a copious amount onto my plate. I liked Aidan, not just for what he could do to my body but the quiet simplicity of his company. He didn't push conversation on me or feel the need to fill the silence. He was happy just to sit there with me. However, his current behavior was worrying.

Swirling a fry in my ketchup, I munched on it. "So, what's up?"

Aidan put his fork down from the spaghetti on his plate and turned his gaze to me. Another thing I loved. He stopped everything to give me his complete attention. "Lunch?"

I lifted a fry up to Aris. She didn't so much as flinch. Frowning, I shoved the fry into my mouth. Maybe she doesn't like French fries? If so, we were gonna have a problem. I turned my attention back to Aidan.

"No, I mean..." I picked up another fry and waved at him. "This. You never used to worry about bothering me. If I do recall, you sought me out more than half the time."

I knew my words were affecting him. His shoulders bunched up, and his eyes darted back to his plate. Trying to lighten the mood, I bumped his shoulder with mine, which did absolutely nothing except to bounce me back off of him. He really was built like an ox.

"I was afraid."

Those three little words from him made my heart stutter. "You were afraid? Why?"

He shifted in his seat, clearly uncomfortable with the question. Someone as big as him probably wasn't afraid often. Especially, with his foresight. When you know what was coming, it was hard to be scared of it.

"You got hurt, and I didn't see it." The gruffness to his voice caused me to lean into him, wrapping my arms around his midsection, well as much as I could manage.

"Aw, Aidan. You can't blame yourself for that. No one could have predicted I'd pass out like that."

"I should have." His eyes tightened, and his lower lip poked out slightly. Oh. My. God. He was pouting. This big lug of a man was pouting. I wanted to pet him and call him a pretty boy, but I had a feeling he wouldn't appreciate that. Instead, I reached up and turned his chin toward me.

"Aidan," I softly murmured, keeping my eyes locked with his. "I don't blame you. I blame myself for getting in over my head, but in any case, I saved someone, so I'm not sorry, and you shouldn't be either."

"But..."

"No." I shook my head, putting my finger against his lips. "I appreciate you worrying for me, but I'm a big girl, I make my own decisions good or bad. You can't hold yourself accountable for those, or you're never going to be happy. Alright?"

Aidan's eyes searched mine before he let out a long breath. "Very well."

"Good." I grinned and then pulled his head down to mine. Pressing my lips to his, I gave him a quick but thorough kiss that had even my head spinning before returning to my own seat. "Now, eat. You'll need the strength for later." I waggled my eyebrows at him suggestively.

A deep chuckle released from his chest and his eyes darkened, so they were a stormy blue. My libido jumped about a foot, and I shimmed in my seat. Down, girl.

We finished our meal in relative silence. I stood to put my tray away, but Aidan took it for me. I smiled at him and took his hand. His large fingers engulfed mine as we walked out of the cafeteria. "Where are you off to?"

"The basement."

"Oh?" I quirked a brow. Aidan and Ian were both part of the Dark Arts major which meant they all worked in the basement level of the campus. I had yet to figure out why. Maybe I could now. "Why can't you work up here? You know, with the living."

"Because our work isn't meant for the light." Aidan started us down the hallway directing us toward my next class. I didn't need to ask him how he knew where I was going. He'd either seen it or memorized my schedule. It didn't bother me either way. It was convenient actually.

I chewed on my bottom lip, contemplating his words. "So, what exactly do the Dark Arts mean? Like hoodoo?"

Aidan's lip quirked up at the edge. "No. Hoodoo is more for the religious types, not what we do."

"And what is it you do?" I leaned against his arm, placing my head on his bicep.

"Death magic. Things that require sacrifices, blood, and darkness." He stopped before my classroom, taking my hand to whirl me to stand before him. "Things that are too dangerous for one such as you."

"What's that supposed to mean?" I huffed, trying to pull my hands back from him but he held tight.

My eyes slid sideways to the ball of light by my head. Aris floated like nothing was happening. Apparently, Aidan wasn't a threat. Not that I thought he was in any case, but it was good to know for sure.

Not at all bothered by my outrage, Aidan drew me closer. "You are the light and all things good. You should not be down in the dark lest it decide to keep you." My shoulders sagged at his words, and I tipped my head back as he leaned down to brush his lips against mine.

I blinked and stepped back before I could let myself get too into it. "Then why do you do it, if it is so bad?"

"It's not bad." Aidan straightened, his hands releasing mine. "It's just... complicated."

"Explain it to me then."

Aidan shook his head. "Not here. Later. I promise."

Pursing my lips, I gave a curt nod. "Fine, but don't think I'll forget." I wagged a finger at him playfully.

"I won't." He smiled and then urged me toward the door. "Go, before you are late."

I moved toward the door, but he called out to me.

"What? I'm going."

"Every other answer is C."

I frowned at him for a moment, not understanding what he was saying. Then my eyes widened as it dawned on me. Giving him a thumbs up, I rushed into my next class. Sometimes it was good to have a boyfriend as a seer.

Regardless of Aidan's heads up, my Charms class was brutal. I had a feeling I got most of them wrong except the ones that Aidan had told me. Really, who made every other answer C? It was like they were trying to trick you. There should be a law against it.

I had hoped that Aidan would be waiting for me outside of my classroom, but I was sadly disappointed. Must have been in his own class still. Not letting his absence put me down any further than I already was, I headed toward my dorm room.

"Come on, Aris." I waved a hand at Aris as if that would make any difference in what the guardian light did. If there was a way to get rid of the ball of light, I didn't know it. If it got really annoying, I guess, I could look it up.

With a sigh, I walked down the hallway. I had one day of finals done and only one left. I might not get valedictorian like in high school, but I wouldn't be getting the dunce cap any time soon either.

When I got to my dorm room, I reached for the door knob, not really paying much mind. I started to open the door but paused when I saw a hair tie around the handle. Brows crunched together, I tried to figure out what exactly it meant until I heard a giggle then a moan from inside. My eyebrows shot to my forehead, and I backed away with a grin. Trina must be in there with Libby.

"We need to redefine what you think I need warning of," I told Aris with a wry grin. The ball of light just hovered there, the cheeky bitch.

Huffing out a sigh, I backed away from the door. While I was glad they were doing well, I really wanted to collapse in my bed and brood for a bit about my day. However, I wasn't about to rain all over their parade with my grumpiness. So, like any good roommate, I turned around and headed for the quad. Maybe a day in the sun would help me out of my funk.

With a goal in mind, I made quick work of the hallway. Before long, I was out in the sun and air. I lifted my hands up above my head and let out a big sigh. Already more relaxed, I searched out a good spot to chill out. The grass outside was already pretty full of students doing exactly the same thing I was planning on doing, unwinding after a long day of finals. I knew most of them tonight and tomorrow night would be unwinding with a drink or two. I hoped I was one of them.

Finding an empty spot, I didn't hesitate to lay back on the grass, my arms out to either side. I let the sun warm me as I pictured myself sinking into the cool ground beneath me. After a few moments, my eyes began to droop. I didn't fight it and let myself snooze. I'd only been out for a few minutes before two bodies took up residence next to me. I smiled as a familiar scent filled my nose, and a hand brushed my hair away from my face.

"I see your potion worked?" Paul's voice came from my left, his arm pressing against my own.

Sighing, I licked my lips. "Yep. I have my very own Tinkerbell now. She's pretty useless actually."

"Tough day?"

I blinked my eyes opened and smiled up at his big brown eyes. "Torturous. How about you?"

"It was alright. Nothing I can't handle." He moved his body closer to mine, and a part of me flushed. Lying next to me, his shirt was pulled tight and showed the lines of his abs beneath. If his proximity wasn't enough to give me flashbacks to our time together, then the hint of what I knew lay beneath his clothing definitely did.

"I bet." My lashes fluttered, and my voice came out breathy. A movement on my other side barely called my attention away from Paul.

"What am I? Chopped liver?" A partially offended voice jerked my eyes from Paul to his brother, Ian. A lopsided grin on his lips, Ian's hazel eyes twinkled with amusement but had an underlying hurt in it.

Well, I knew how to fix that.

Sliding my leg over his, I grabbed the front of his shirt and jerked his mouth to my own. Not caring who was looking, I slipped my tongue between his lips and tangled it with his own. Pulling the appendage into my mouth to suck on it a moment, I didn't stop until Ian let out a heady moan.

Releasing his mouth, I wiped the edges of my lips with the pad of my thumb and smirked. "Better?"

Clearing his throat and adjusting himself, Ian chuckled. "Yeah, but now I have a hard-on."

I couldn't stop my eyes from drifting down to his lap where a prominent bulge showed beneath his jeans, and I licked my lips.

Ian groaned and buried his face in my shoulder. "Please, stop. You're killing me."

Paul's hand trailed up the back of my neck and tugged on my ponytail. "Maybe you'd like to head back to your room?"

I gasped at the implications but then sighed. "I'd love to, but Trina's currently having her own alone time in there."

"We could go back to my room," Paul suggested, his fingers curling along my hip, his front pushed up against my ass, letting me know he was just as excited to see me as his brother.

"As much as I'd love to join in this weird threesome, I have to get back." Ian stood before I could protest. Brushing the grass off his jeans, he squatted next to me, his fingers cupping my chin. "I'll text you later, k?"

Nodding but frowning, I watched Ian walk back toward the school. When he was out of sight, I turned to Paul. "What's going on with him?"

Paul shrugged slightly, his mouth going to trail along the shell of my ear. "How should I know?"

"You're his brother, duh."

"So?" Paul lifted his head, his brows scrunched between his eyes. "He doesn't talk to me like that. You're better off pumping Aidan for information than me." He paused for a second as I arched a brow at him. "Actually, you're right. If you are going to pump anyone, it should be me."

I threw my head back and laughed, shoving him away a bit. "You're such a perv. I'm not pumping anyone for information. I just want to know why Ian's acting like he has better things to do than spend time with me." My lips curved down and heaved a sigh.

"He's not. Trust me." Paul rolled me over to face him, his eyes soft. "If he could, he'd be here with you right now, even if it was to have a threesome with his brother."

I smiled despite myself. "You know, that's kind of a fetish."

"What is?"

"Brothers."

The smile on Paul's face spread wide. "Oh, really now? You want a brother sandwich?"

I nodded, biting the inside of my cheek to keep from laughing. "Even better if they're twins."

"Someone has been watching too much porn." Paul poked my forehead with his finger and moved back. Standing, he offered me a hand. "Come on, I have just enough time to rock your world before I have to go help grade papers."

Rolling my eyes, I took his hand. "Such a romantic gesture. A quickie between classes."

Paul winked. "You know me, all about the romance."

Remembering the way he had made love to me in the Potions lab caused my core to warm. Oh, yes, he knew romance. If only he didn't get jealous of the other guys so easily.

The fact that he hadn't said anything yet today about it was a miracle in itself.

Instead of going back through the quad, Paul directed me toward the front of the school. We began to cross the circular driveway they had for picking up and dropping off people when Aris started to freak out. I paused to look up at her when a white Jeep came zooming around the corner, stopping right in front of us. I jumped back, holding onto Paul's arm.

"What's your problem?" Paul shouted at the driver, his arm in front of me protectively. When a familiar blonde head popped out of the side of the car, I knew why my Guardian Light was on high alert.

"Jesus fucking Christ, Sabrina, did all that bleach finally go to your brain?" I snarled at her still behind the steering wheel as I moved Paul's arm out of my way. "You could have hit us."

"Sorry," she said in a sing-song voice, a bit of a bite to her words. I thought that was the end of it, but Sabrina didn't get out or anything. She just stared at me.

"What? Do I have something on my face?"

Sabrina sighed dramatically, tapping her perfectly manicured nails on the jeep. "Are you going to get in or what? I don't have all day."

Paul and I turned to each other at the same time, our faces both relaying a 'what the fuck' message. Turning back to Sabrina, I shook my head. "I'm not going anywhere with you."

"Oh, come on. Be a grown-up." She scoffed and shook her head. "I don't want to do this any more than you. Just get in the damn car."

"I seriously have no idea what you are talking about." Just then my phone buzzed in my pocket. Pulling it out, I read the caller ID before answering. What were the chances? "Grandmother, hello."

"Maxine, darling. I meant to call you earlier but was held up with other matters. How are you?" My grandmother, Mistress Mancaster, sounded just as dignified and put together on the phone as she did in real life. She'd make the President's wife cry of envy with how easily she handled everything that was thrown at her. Well, everything except my harem of wizards. That one I got an earful for.

"I'm alright." I shifted from one foot to the other, my eyes going to Paul. He still had a confused expression, and I shrugged. "I'm trying to figure out why Sabrina Craftsman is demanding I get in her car. So, if she kidnaps me, this is my notice for you to call the authorities."

I was joking. Kind of. For all I knew Sabrina would kidnap me one of these days, torturing me for daring to defy her.

My grandmother made a startled noise. "My apologies. I had hoped to get a hold of you before Ms. Craftsman approached you. That is entirely my fault."

"So, you know about this?" I arched a brow at Paul, who seemed to be catching on a whole of a lot faster than me.

"Yes, of course. I arranged it."

I made a rude sound through my nose. "Why the ever loving he... ck would you do that?" I caught myself before I started to curse up a storm. Grandmother already thought I was an uncouth hoodlum no need to add to it.

"It's customary for you to have a senior witch help you through the steps of your coming out," she continued. "I thought since Ms. Craftsman is in the same year as you, the two of you might have something in common. Besides, her family is one of the most prestigious in the area. You couldn't ask for a better sister witch to assist you."

Fucking A. I wasn't going to be able to get out of this.

"Are you sure this is necessary?" I asked her as Sabrina honked the horn, causing Paul and me to wince. I flipped her off as I plugged my other ear. "I think I can manage this all on my own."

"Nonsense. Ms. Craftsman is a lovely young lady, and you should strive to follow her example." I forced back the snort at her words. The day I followed Sabrina's example would be the day I wore my panties on my head and squawked like a bird. "Now, I hope to hear good reports on what you decide. Bye."

She hung up before I could get another word in edgewise. Scowling down at the phone, I shoved it into my pocket before I chunked it across the lawn.

"I'm guessing we're not going to my room then?" Paul asked, a dejected expression on his face.

Frowning, I took his hands in mine. "Sorry, apparently Sabrina has been selected as my torturer for the coming out party. I wasn't given the option to decline."

Paul gave me a sympathetic smile. "It's alright. I have pushy parents too. Rain check?"

"Oh, you better believe it." I inched up and pressed my lips to his, letting myself sink into his embrace.

I'd barely gotten into that kiss before the horn blared again and Sabrina shouted, "Stop sucking face, witch. We're going shopping!"

Chapter 4

I SAT IN SABRINA'S car with a perpetual scowl on my lips. I didn't trust her. Not with my life, hell not even with a stray cat I found on the street. I certainly didn't trust that she was helping me out of the goodness of her little black heart.

"Why are you doing this?" I held onto the door handle and gave her a sideways glance. "What's in it for you?"

"What makes you think I'm doing this for you?" Sabrina snorted, never taking her eyes off the road. For a prissy bitch, at least she was a decent driver. Her long blonde hair sat over her shoulder and looked like she had gotten a blowout recently. Knowing her personality, she probably got one every week.

"Then who are you doing it for?"

Sabrina put her foot on the clutch and switched gears, barely giving me a look.

"Your grandmother called my mother and asked me to be your big sister. Of course, I couldn't say no."

"Sure, you can. No. See? That easy." I clenched my teeth into a tight sardonic grin. Aris wasn't much help. She wasn't bothered by the fact that Sabrina had practically kidnapped me. Of course, I got into her car on my own, but it wasn't like I had much of a choice.

Rolling her eyes, Sabrina pulled into the parking lot of the mall. "You know good and well that I can't just say no. It's not done."

"That's just stupid."

"Says you." Sabrina found a parking spot and turned to glower at me. "You didn't grow up with your parents breathing down your neck, watching your every move to make sure you acted exactly according to their plan for you. If you so much as try to revolt, they threaten to kick you out, cutting you off from your friends, family, and everything you hold dear." She grabbed her purse from the back seat and settled me with a strange look of envy. "Count yourself lucky."

I stared at where Sabrina sat for a few moments. What the heck? Had I misjudged this stuck-up witch for someone who actually was worth befriending? I mean, if I had been in her shoes, would I have turned out the same way? Guilt started to eat at my stomach for the way I had acted toward her.

A bang on the window made me jerk in my seat. "Hurry up. I have better places to be than babysitting you."

Then again, some people were just jerk faces no matter their upbringing.

Taking my sweet time getting out of the car, I followed Sabrina into the mall. I paused in place for a second. "Hold on. What about this thing?" I pointed at Aris. "Won't people see her?"

Sabrina turned back to me and gave Aris the stink eye. "Stop referring to it as a she. It's not sentient, and humans can't see it unless you tell them. So, just ignore it, and no one will be the wiser."

Pouting, I told Aris, "Ignore her. She doesn't know what the hell she's talking about." Scurrying after Sabrina, I tried not to look at Aris, though it was hard not to.

"What exactly are we here for?" It was the middle of the week and almost three o'clock, meaning the mall was full of students having just gotten out of school. It made maneuvering through the mall a bit difficult especially when my guide wasn't bothering to notice if I was keeping up.

"If I'm going to be your" - Sabrina shuddered as if it actually physically affected her - "big sister witch, then I have to know what I'm dealing with. So, to get a feel for..." She spun around and waved hand up and down my jeans and t-shirt clad form. "... your look, I need to see you shop."

I grimaced.

"Do we have to?" I searched around the mall for something to distract her. "Can't we just buy a pretzel and bitch about our parents?"

Sabrina actually gave me a genuine smile. "Maybe later. First, shoes!"

She put one hand on her hip and pointed a finger towards the shoe store. I had a vision of her in her own superhero movie. She'd be Mall Girl. Or Witch Bitch. Something like that. And her powers would be throwing stiletto heels at her enemies and slicing them with her cutting words.

"Are you coming?"

I jolted out of my fantasy and hurried after her with a sigh. I gave up sex with Paul for shopping. This was going to be a long afternoon.

Several grueling hours later, I was ready to kill Sabrina and myself. "Are we done yet?"

"Not until I know you aren't going to reflect badly on me because of your poor choices. Now..." She held up two dresses one that was a silky blood red color and the other an emerald green of the same material. "Which one would you wear to an evening out with your," she paused for a moment and then bit out, "boyfriend?"

I quirked a smile. "Which one?"

Dropping her arms with a scowl, Sabrina tsked. "This is serious, Max. Your choice in an outfit will make or break your coming out. This will announce you to all the magical community. You don't want to give them the wrong impression, do you?"

I knew what I wanted to answer, but I also knew that telling her what was really on my mind would only make us stand in this store for another three hours.

Sighing and trying to hold back the need to jam a fork in my eye, I said, "No..."

"No, what?"

Wrinkling my nose, I stared up at her. She crossed her arms over her chest and stared at me. "No, big sister." Man, that tasted putrid in my mouth.

"Good. Now, which one?" She held the two dress back up.

"I would wear the red one for a night out with my boyfriend."

"And the other one?"

"For dinner with my family."

"Or?" she arched a brow.

"Or with other acquaintances." When Sabrina gave me a satisfied smirk, I sagged. "Are we done now? I'm starving."

"Fine, but the pretzel place is closed now." She handed the dresses back to the clerk who glared at Sabrina behind her back. I'd be pissed too. We spent hours in her store trying on everything imaginable and weren't going to leave with a single purchase.

Feeling bad for the clerk, I handed her a dark blue bra and panties set that had light blue lining and a bow in the middle. "Can you ring this up for me, please?"

Giving me a grateful smile, the clerk took the set up to the counter.

"The pretzel place would have been open had we not spent the whole time in this store," I pointed out. "Really, I'm not sure this is what my grandmother meant when she asked for your help."

Sabrina sniffed and pulled her purse over her shoulder. "Well, I agreed to do this, so I'm going to do it my way. If you choose the wrong thing, then people will talk, and you'll get ostracized before you even debut."

"When did you start to care about what I do? Wouldn't you be happy if everyone hated me?" I stood from the seat by the changing room, wincing at the aches in my body. Who knew trying on clothes could be so tiring?

"Because, as your sister witch, your choices reflect onto me. If you pick badly, then it makes me look bad." She stopped talking as the clerk came back with my bag. I handed her my card and thanked her. "Who's that for?" Sabrina wagged her finger at my small bag. "Paul?"

I lifted a shoulder, not really comfortable talking about her ex-boyfriend, now my boyfriend, with her. "I don't know. Maybe. I just thought it was cute."

She hummed as if she didn't quite believe me, then asked, "How do you juggle all four of them? I mean, I have a hard enough time getting one guy to do what I ask, let alone four."

I laughed. "Well, I can't say I have a lot of experience with juggling boyfriends. Before them, I only had the one serious one."

"Really?" Sabrina scanned over me, critiquing my every attribute. "I find that hard to believe. I can't see how you wouldn't have had more. You obviously have something guys can't resist, or you wouldn't have so many now."

"Believe me, if I knew, I'd tell you." When the clerk came back, I took my card back from her and headed for the door. "I didn't exactly sing a siren call to make them all fall for me, and I certainly didn't set out to date so many. I have enough on my plate as it is."

"Then why date them all at all?" Sabrina walked side by side with me for once, not ordering me around like her servant. "If it's so much trouble."

"It's not really. I mean, yeah there's been a bit of jealousy and having to make sure I'm being fair, but overall, it's been... fun. The guys all provide me with something different." I shrugged, not sure if I made much sense to her, let alone to myself.

Sabrina was quiet as if mulling over my words. She didn't speak again until we got into her car. "And what about sex?"

"What about it?" I glanced over at her, expecting her to say something rude at any moment.

For once, Sabrina seemed uncomfortable with the subject even though she had brought it up. "Do you, you know, do them all together?"

I stared at her for a moment and then laughed, my head back and my hand slapping my thigh.

"Fine. If you're going to be a bitch about it, forget it." She turned with a huff, cranking her car.

"I'm sorry," I hurried to say, placing a hand on her arm. "Really, I just didn't expect you to say that. I'm not making fun of you."

"Whatever."

"For real." I stared her down, and she finally seemed to relent as she pulled out of the parking lot. "Look, I don't know really what I'm doing. I certainly haven't slept with them all at once and don't plan to... at least I don't think." My brow scrunched in thought. "I wouldn't even begin to figure out the mechanics that would require. Besides, I've only had sex with Paul."

"So, how's that fair?" she asked, genuinely seeming interested. "You slept with Paul, excellent choice by the way, but not the others? Aren't they upset by that?"

I shook my head. "I'm not going to push myself to do it with the others until I'm ready just to save their egos. If it comes down to that, they can just fuck off." Sabrina giggle-snorted at that, making me smile. "Besides, it's not like I haven't done anything with the others. I just haven't gone all the way."

"I've only ever dated one person seriously," Sabrina confessed as we drove. "I mean, I've dated, and I've slept with, well, obviously you know about Paul and Ian, but there were a few others. I'm not some big slut or anything, and save for that little indiscretion with Ian, they were all when Paul and I were broken up."

I frowned. "So, Paul's the only guy you were serious about?"

She gave me a sideways look. "Our parents have pushed us at each other ever since we were in diapers. I couldn't really tell them no."

"Except when he doesn't want to date you anymore," I pointed out, not wanting to be a bitch but really wanting to know how she was going to handle that. "What do they think of that?"

"Well, I haven't exactly told them... yet." Sabrina stared straight ahead to avoid my gaze. When she saw my 'what the fuck' look I was giving her, she rolled her eyes. "I'm not holding out for him to take me back. We all know that ship has sailed, but bringing things up like this is a delicate situation. It'll be easier to break their hearts if I have someone even better to take Paul's place."

"And that's all that matters?" I asked, feeling a bit sorry for her. "That your parents are happy? What about you?"

"What about me?" She sniffed. "I will get my inheritance when I turn twenty-one and then I can do whatever the hell I want. So, if that means playing by their rules for a bit longer, I will."

"Don't you want to fall in love?"

She laughed, but it sounded bitter. "When you belong to one of the most powerful magical families in Georgia, you don't get to think about things like love. You'll learn that too, once you give up on your human side."

"I won't though," I argued, not believing for a second that I would ever do that to myself.

"You will," she said with a soft sigh. "Just watch. It'll start with something small, and then each little compromise will find you somewhere else. Next thing you know, you're doing things for the sake of your family name without even questioning your own happiness."

I didn't like what she was implying. I couldn't imagine myself ever being that way. I was too headstrong for one. For another, I knew my mother wouldn't let me accept anything that might harm me emotionally. The fact that she hadn't pitched a complete fit about the coming out party told me she didn't find it to be that bad. I could only hope that my grandmother wouldn't try to find another way around her.

"So, have you thought about who you are going to have escort you?" Sabrina eventually asked as we pulled into the school's parking lot.

I shook my head. "No, I haven't. If I pick just one of them, then they might think I'm playing favorites. However, if I go alone..."

"Don't even think about it," Sabrina interrupted with a growl. "If you show up alone, it will be social suicide. Trust me. This one witch, Jessica, didn't have an escort, and now you know where she is?"

"Happier for it?" I guessed.

"Nowhere. That's where. No one knows what happened to her, and all because she went stag to her own party. You don't want that on your record, especially since you already have so many strikes against you just by being human-raised."

"There's the Sabrina I love to hate. This whole nice thing was creeping me out." I gave a nervous chuckle.

"Well, don't get used to it. We aren't friends. I'm not going to braid your hair or sit with you during breaks." She scowled at me, putting her car in park. "Now get out of my car. I'll text you to meet again."

"But you don't have my number."

"Your grandmother gave it to me already." She said as if I should have known it. "Now don't too excited. And don't be one of those people who send me dog pictures or whatever. I hate animals."

I rolled my eyes. "I'm sure you do. Well, this has been... interesting, but I'm going to go now."

"Didn't I just say that?" she scoffed and pulled out her phone, typing away and ignoring me. Taking that as my cue to leave, I climbed out of the car and walked quickly toward the school.

I hadn't lied when I said my time with Sabrina had been interesting. I'd learned quite a few things about the magical community that I knew I would have messed up on my own. I also learned Sabrina wasn't as bad as she tried to pretend to be. I wasn't saying we were going to be best friends, but maybe, eventually, we wouldn't be trying to hex each other's eyes out at every turn which in my book was a win.

"What do you think, Aris?" I asked my Guardian light. It just hovered there in the air. "Yep, I agree. She's still a bitch, but at least she's on our side now."

Chapter 5

LAYING IN MY BED, I went over the events of the day, many of which I didn't quite understand myself. Libby had long since left thankfully. I'd had quite enough of other people for the day. Even Trina had caught onto my mood and had taken her books to the library to study rather than sit in the room.

Sighing, I rolled over in my bed, and my eyes caught sight of the little bag holding my new underwear set. I threw my legs over the side of my bed and picked it up. Pulling the tags off, I sat it on the bed next to me while I shimmied out of my clothes.

When I had the new set on, I stood in front of the mirror hanging on the back of the closet. It was pretty enough. My breasts were large as it was, and the bra only accentuated them. I was happy to have picked one without a push-up part, or my breasts would have been up to my ears and falling out every two seconds. There were few good things about being well endowed, and being able to find cute bras was one of the downsides.

"What do you think?" I asked Aris. "Think this will knock the socks off the guys?" I paused for a moment and then giggled to myself. "You're right. More like it'll knock their pants off."

As my eyes skimmed over the thin straps of the panties, a knock came to my door. Jumping in place, I covered my hands over myself. Then I remembered, duh, the door was closed so whoever was there couldn't see me.

"Who is it?"

"It's Dale. Can I come in?" His scratchy voice came through the wood of the door.

I started to tell him to come in and then stopped. Taking a look at myself again, I knew what answering the door in this would seem like. Was I ready to take that step with Dale? I meant what I said to Sabrina. I wasn't going to force myself to have sex with any of them before I was ready. I thought about Dale waiting on the other side of the door, his cute freckled face, the glasses he couldn't stop pushing up his nose, and the tight body I knew laid beneath his clothing.

Yep. I was ready, or at least my body was. It wasn't like we hadn't practically had sex already. Though fooling around in the shower was hardly what anyone would call sex.

"Max?"

"Uh, yeah. Come in," I called out, my hands opening and closing at my sides. I wasn't sure what to do with them. Should I strike a sexy pose or something?

I didn't have time to decide before the door opened. Dale poked his head in first, his eyes moving over the room before landing on my underwear-clad form. His eyes widened, and he pushed his glasses up his face before hurrying inside.

Breathing a bit quicker than normal, I waited to see his reaction. We'd danced around the subject of sex, and he'd never tried to force me, but I really wanted to know what he was thinking. Was I wrong in assuming he'd want to?

"Wow," Dale breathed out, his eyes scanning over my body, lingering over my bare thighs. "You look... wow." Licking his lips, his lust-filled eyes lifted to mine. "Is this all for me?"

I shifted in place, my foot trailing along the carpet. "If you want it to be." I peered up at him beneath my lashes, my arms behind my back as I swayed from side to side.

"Oh, yes, I do." Dale took a step closer until we were within touching distance. He didn't waste any time, his hands coming around my waist and pulling me up against him.

I pressed up on my toes, brushing my nose against his before kissing him. A low moan escaped as his hand cupped the back of my neck and his tongue played with mine. A thought came to me, and I pulled away suddenly. At Dale's confused expression, I smiled.

"The door?"

"Oh. Gotcha."

I slipped past him, putting an extra sway in my hips as I went to the door and locked it. Turning back around, I put my back to the door. "Do you know the spell to do that cone of silence thing?"

Dale cocked a brow. "Yeah, sure, but you know you have to do it, or it won't work."

I slid one leg against the other calling his eyes down to them. "I know, but I thought you might teach me how."

If anything, the bulge in Dale's pants grew larger at the thought of teaching me something. I laughed on the inside. He was such a nerd.

"I'd be happy to." Dale moved over to me, caging me in between him and the door. His head dipped down, and his mouth nipped at my lips. "First, you want to imagine a bubble inside your head." One hand left the door, and his fingers trailed along the lining of the cup of my bra. "Do you have your bubble?"

My breath hitched, and I swallowed, shaking my head.

Dale smirked. "Close your eyes." I did. "Now, picture a bubble, round and firm." His hand cupped my breast as he spoke, and all my thoughts went out the window. His finger dipped into my bra, tweaking the nipple. "Are you focusing?"

"Yes," I squeaked out.

"I don't think you are."

"Well, can you blame me?" I gasped as he pinched the tip of my breast. Shimming in place, I straightened back up. "Fine, fine. I'm envisioning a bubble. Does it matter the color?" I peeked an eye open, but Dale wasn't looking at my face. "Dale?"

Dale's lips curled into a wolfish grin, his eyes moving from my nipple to my face. "Pink, a lovely flesh pink."

I snorted but did as he asked. "Now what?"

"Now, push it out." Dale pulled the cup of my bra down my breast popping out of the confines. "Push until it covers the entire room." His hand lifted my breast and brought it to his mouth.

As the hot cavern of his mouth covered my breast, I focused on not making a sound until I had pushed the bubble to the max. "Now what?" I panted, turning my head to the side.

Dale let go of my breast with a pop. "Now, you let go." His hand slid between my thighs and stroked the front of my new panties, already soaked through by his actions.

My head fell back, and I let out a long, heady moan. Dale's finger hooked inside the bottom of the material, rubbing along my flesh and entrance. I bucked against his hand and grabbed at his hair, urging him to give me more.

"Like that?"

I nodded, unable to form words.

"Good." Dale grinned before taking his finger away and pulling my panties down my legs. The cool air touched my aching core, and I pressed my thighs together, seeking to subdue the need inside me.

"Now, don't do that," Dale said, kneeling before me, his hands urging my legs back apart. "I'm not done with you yet." He picked one leg up and pulled it over his shoulder before burying his face between my thighs.

My eyes rolled back into my head as he lapped at me. I tangled my fingers in his hair holding on for dear life, my heart pounding in my chest a million miles a minute. I was embarrassed to say it didn't take me long to get off, and Dale was back on his feet a smug grin on his lips.

"Well," I breathed heavily, my eyes hooded as I peered up at him. "That was... wow."

Dale wrapped his arms around my waist and drew me toward the bed. "If you think that was good, the best has yet to come." He wagged his brows at me.

I giggled and climbed onto the bed with him. Settling into his lap, I unsnapped my bra and tossed it aside. Dale's eyes went straight to my chest, the hands on my waist moving up to cup my breasts.

Pulling my lower lip between my teeth, I made quick work of the buttons of his shirt. I paused in my trek to undress him and Dale frowned.

Ignoring his displeasure, I eyed Aris. "You should probably close your eyes. This isn't a free show."

The pale ball of light just stared at me.

Dale's fingers slid along the skin at my hips. "Are you really worried about your guardian watching us have sex?"

My forehead crinkled. "I don't know how advanced she is. Aris could be rubbing one out right now, getting off on all this delicious muscle." I leaned down and licked his abs, the muscles under my hands tensing. I eyed him beneath my lashes. "She's such a little pervert."

Dale chuckled breathily.

As I pushed the edges of his shirt open further, I raked my fingers all along his chest and abs until my finger trailed down his happy trail and released him from his pants.

Dale's eyelids drooped as I groped him, sliding my hand up and down his length. Swirling a finger around the tip, I couldn't take my eyes off Dale's expression. Watching this powerful wizard come undone beneath my hands made my chest swell with pride, even more so when he gripped my hand and begged me to stop.

"Why? Don't you like it?" I asked coyly, blinking big innocent eyes up at him. "From the sounds you were making, I thought differently."

Letting out a breathy laugh, Dale slid his hands beneath my ass lifting me up. "Oh, believe me, I enjoyed it but not as much as I will enjoy this." He sank me down onto his length, and my head fell back with a gasp. My nails dug into his shoulders as I let out an exquisite hiss. Dale swallowed and met my gaze. "Alright there?"

Licking my lips, I nodded.

Sliding his hands up the length of my back, his eyes narrowed behind his glasses. I had a feeling the way he looked at me was the same way he looked at a math problem or a particularly hard charm. The intensity of it only made it that much better. When we moved, all my thoughts went out the window, and the only things that were left were the sensations he brought to me.

Pressing my forehead to his, my hips undulated against him our breathing coming in faster the more we moved. And with that act, the air thickened with almost electric tension. The hairs on my arms stood on end, and every brush of our skin caused a rush of little electric shocks.

"What's happening?" I stuttered out and then when Dale shifted his hips in a particular way, I whimpered. Oh, yes. A good study, this one. For a moment I forgot my question and what was happening even when the desk shook, and my lamp fell off the end. My cries came out sharper, and Dale muttered something. "Wh-what?"

"Magic," Dale groaned out, his teeth clenched, his hands gripping my back tightly. By the erratic movement of his hips,

Dale must have been close. I wasn't that far away as it was.

The bed banged against the dorm room wall, and I startled, gripping Dale's arms. "Wa-wait." Fuck. That was good. "Shouldn't we be... uh... worried?" I shot a look to Aris, who didn't seem worried at all. Of course, with this much sexiness available to gawk at, I wouldn't be doing my job either.

Dale chuckled and paused his thrusts long enough to stroke the side of my face. "As a witch, if you don't break at least a few pieces of furniture, it means the sex was bad."

Laughing with him, I bent my head to capture his lips with mine while he resumed our movements. This time when the bed shook, I shoved Dale, so he lay on his back. My hands planted on either side of his head, I grinned down at his bemused eyes. Pulling my lower lip between my teeth, I rocked my hips, and the bed moved with it. It was a good thing I had the cone of silence on because the bed banged against the wall with each thrust of my hips and it was oh so good.

When we both reached our climax and collapsed in a heap on my bed, I finally spoke again. "Well, that was interesting. I half expected us to end up on the ceiling or something."

Dale chuckled, turning on his side to look at me. "That could be arranged."

"Really?" My eyebrows rose at his smirk. I stroked the arm that laid across my hips. "What else?"

"What else have I done?"

"Yeah. I've only been with..." I trailed off and flushed. "Well, you, Paul, and my ex-boyfriend from high school, and he was human, so not a whole lot of magical sex experience." I chewed on my lower lip, not sure if he would want to answer my next question. "What about you?"

"What about me?" I gave him a meaningful look, and his eyes widened slightly, his lips parting to form an o shape. Then a slow sexy smile slid up his lips. "Why, Ms. Norman, are you asking about my past lovers?"

I ducked my head, grinning as I focused on the hair on his arm. "Maybe. Okay, yes. But can you blame me?"

"Relax." Dale brushed my hair away from my face. "It's fine. You can ask." He didn't say anything else after that, so I shook his arm.

"Come on, don't leave me in suspense."

"I said you could ask, I didn't say I would answer." The laughter in his voice made me shove him.

"Now that's not nice."

"Oh, alright." Dale sighed and rolled over. Getting out of the bed, his eyes scanned over my nude form as he pulled his jeans back on. "I've dated several people since I hit puberty. Some were lovers, others not."

Leaning up on my elbow, I arched a brow. "People? As in…" A slow smile spread across my face.

"Women, you naughty girl." He leaned onto the bed with his hands, his nose brushing mine. His breath kissed my lips, but he only teased. "I've never been with a man, but I'm not opposed to sharing. Just don't ask me to suck anyone off."

I threw my head back and laughed. "I wouldn't dream of it." This time Dale raised a brow at me. "Okay, maybe I do sometimes, but I would never ask you to do something you're not comfortable with."

"And I, you." Dale pulled his shirt on, buttoning it up. "So, I heard you went shopping with Sabrina Craftsman today? How did that happen?"

Rolling my eyes, I flopped back down on the bed. "Ugh, don't even start. It wasn't my idea."

"Let me guess, your grandmother?"

I turned my head toward him. "She's supposed to be my big sister witch or some other bullshit. You know, for the coming out party?"

Dale's nose crinkled at the mention of the party. "I'm assuming that, as your boyfriend, I am expected to attend this social gathering?"

I snorted and sat up. "You sound about as thrilled as I do about having to be the guest of honor. At least you can wear a suit. I'm sure I'll be stuck in some big fluffy monstrosity." I threw my legs over the side of the bed, not at all bothered at being naked in front of him. When did I get so comfortable in my own skin?

Tying the last laces of his shoes, Dale grabbed my hands and pulled me up and into his arms. One hand behind my head, he murmured, "As long as I can tear it off of you at the end of the night, I'm in." His mouth captured mine in a searing kiss that left my toes curling and eager to pull him back into bed. When he released me, I found my legs a bit wobbly, but Dale kept moving toward the door.

"Where are you going?" Disappointment spread through my chest, a slight sting of insecurity wiggling inside.

Dale tossed me a grin and a wink. "Finals tomorrow. Have to study up."

"Like you don't already have it all memorized." I stuck my tongue out at him. "Maybe you could spend a bit longer memorizing something else." My eyes dropped down as I moved my fingers along my thighs, tempting him to stay.

The sound Dale made was of a dying man struggling for a grip on life, or at least, I'd like to think so. When I looked up at him, he was two feet closer and one shirt fewer.

"How can I refuse an offer like that?" Dale almost ripped his jeans getting them off, making me grin.

"What about your finals?" I giggled as he scooped me back into his arms. "Don't you need to study."

Dale's hand caressed my lower back before dipping down to my ass giving it a good squeeze. "Like you said, I already have it all memorized. I'm up for a new challenge."

Chapter 6

FINALS WERE FINALLY OVER. I wasn't sure if I had passed them all on a level I was used to, but I knew I had done my best. Fortunately, with finals over, that meant it was time for the end of the year party.

"It's mainly just an excuse to get shit faced and screw," Trina told me with a grin, pulling on her knee-high stockings. They were a bright neon orange color and went well with the dark purple jumper she wore. Trina did not have a confidence issue, that was for sure. I'd never be brave enough to wear something that screamed 'look at me' like that. At least, not to a party of people I didn't know. Usually, Callie had to force me into something other than a cute outfit and into something more adult.

"Well, I, for one, am excited." Paul bounced on my bed slightly with a grin on his face. I was still bummed we had gotten interrupted by my impromptu shopping spree with Sabrina. However, I had a feeling Paul was hoping we'd get to finish what we started tonight. I knew I was.

I offered him a small smile, looping my hoop earring into my ear. "Well, as long as you don't give me any Bubble Pop, I think we'll all have a fun time."

Trina and Paul laughed at that. The last party I'd gone to, I'd let myself get shit faced after one drink. Who knew magical alcohol was so much stronger than regular? Dale did, that's who. I tried not to think of the reason Dale had given me that drink in the first place. Paul and I had been great ever since we had cleared up the misunderstanding between us, and I didn't want to let thoughts of that night ruin tonight's fun.

"So, what are you wearing?" Trina asked me, standing from her bed to come to my side by our full-length mirror.

I raised a brow and gestured to myself. "This."

Trina's eyes took in my low-rise jeans and the tank top with thin straps and a cute bow on the neckline. "Oh, come on, this is a party, shake things up a bit!" She shook my hips, making me laugh. I pushed her hands away, but before I could defend my clothing choice, Paul spoke up.

"I like what you're wearing." Paul gave me a lopsided grin that made his brown eyes twinkle. "Besides, it's only going to end up on the floor later anyway."

My face flushed and my whole body sizzled with a sudden need. Sure, I'd just been with Dale last night, but this was Paul. Sure, I know what you're thinking. All dicks are the same, but they're not. Each of my guys was different and while I hadn't been with all of them yet, something I wasn't in a hurry to do, I had a feeling every one of them would be different.

"Is it hot in here or is it just me?" Trina fanned herself with a giggle, eyeing Paul and me. I ducked my head slightly in embarrassment at being caught eye fucking Paul but didn't comment. Trina didn't wait for one in any case. She grabbed her phone and shoved it between her boobs before heading for the door. "Well, Libby is waiting for me. We already planned on going back to her room this time so no worries about coming back here. You two play nice now. Or not." She shrugged. "Whatever gets you off."

Laughing as she left, I shook my head. I loved my roommate, but sometimes, she could really be something else. I turned back to Paul to ask him about tonight, but my words caught in my throat at the heat in his eyes. Shifting in place, I suddenly felt on the spot. Should I come to him or stay where I was? Should I break the growing sexual tension between us to get to the party? Really, there should be a rule book out there for this kind of stuff.

"Come here," Paul said, saving me from making the decision.

I moved from one foot to the other for a moment before walking toward him. My hands played with my sides as my nerves kicked in. Why was I so nervous? We'd already done it before. What happened to the confidence I had yesterday when I was practically dry humping him in the quad? Hell if I knew, but I demanded yesterday me come back and play the sexy vixen she's supposed to be.

Paul's hands dragged me to him the moment I came within reach. Fingers slid beneath the fabric of my tank top, tickling the edges of my skin. I placed my hands on his shoulders and bent my head toward his, allowing our mouths to match up. Our lips brushed against one another slowly at first before Paul opened his lips and swiped his tongue along my closed mouth. I readily parted them for him with a small groan. His grip tightened on my waist and drew me even closer so that I had to make a choice, stand between his legs or over them. I chose the latter.

Throwing my legs over each of his, I straddled his lap, causing our middles to grind against one another. Paul's fingers inched down from my back to cup my ass and pull me firmly against him.

"I don't think I can wait until after the party," Paul murmured against my lips in between hot, open mouth kisses on my bare neck and shoulders.

"Then don't," I cried out as he nipped my skin. There she was. My nerves had completely vanished, leaving me with nothing but a need to be closer to Paul. I pulled at his shirt, finding the bottom of it so I could run my hands along his hard muscles. His abs tensed at my touch and then when my fingers dipped lower, Paul let out a low, strangled moan.

"Max," he gasped, his fingers tangling in my hair and dragging my mouth back down to his. I made quick work of his pants, but just as I was about to release him from his pants, a quick knock came to my door. Before I had a chance to answer it, the door opened.

"Who's ready to party?" I jerked back from Paul's mouth as Ian's voice filled the room, and my head swiveled toward him. When his eyes landed on us, he paused in his tracks, his eyes wide and a slow smirk crawling up his face. "Well, it looks like someone has already started without us."

A gruff sound came from the hallway, and Ian moved aside to let Aidan through the door. Before I could make an uncomfortable situation worse, I climbed out of Paul's lap, the movement causing a slight sound from both of us, him more than me as his arousal was clear to the rest of the room.

"Hey, we were just..." I started to come up with some excuse but then realized I was being silly. I didn't need to make up stuff for them. We were all adults. They knew I did stuff with Paul the same as with them. "Well, you know," I ended lamely with a giggle.

"Yeah, we can see that." Ian, not giving a fuck about the situation, plopped down on the bed next to his brother and smacked him on the back. "Come on, no hogging the lady. The night is young, and I, for once, have plenty of time to woo and deflower my girl." He wagged his brows at me, making me roll my eyes and giggle again.

"Sorry to tell you, but someone already beat you to that." I crinkled my nose at him.

Ian turned his eyes to Paul who held his hands up. "Don't look at me." He turned his eyes back to me and placed his hands over his heart with woe in my eyes. "You wound me, Max. Not only did you not get deflowered by my brother but by some stranger? Some unworthy human I should guess?"

Covering my mouth to hide my laughter, I nodded.

Slumping down onto the floor, Ian flopped his arm at his sides. "I am beyond repair. Nothing will save my broken heart now."

I arched a brow at him and then at Aidan. Aidan shrugged. Well, he was a lot of help. Glancing back to Ian and then at the clock, I noticed we were already missing all the festivities.

"Well, I don't know about you, but I'm going to go find me a drink." I walked toward the door, stepping over Ian as I went. Paul and Aidan began to follow suit, causing Ian to lift his head.

"You can't just leave me here."

"Why not?" I asked, my hand holding onto the door. "You're the one who said no one could help you. I know a lost cause when I see one." I shifted to leave, but Ian stretched out a hand toward me.

"Wait, there is something. Something you can do to save me."

One hand on my hip, I couldn't keep the sarcasm from my voice. "Oh, really now. And what's that?"

Ian grinned. "A blow job?"

To the guys, I said, "Let's go." Aidan walked out, and Paul followed, but Ian shouted before I could close the door behind us. "What now?"

"Okay, maybe not a blow job, but how about a kiss? A kiss from the fair maiden who has wounded me so?" He blinked his long dark lashes at me, not fair really, and rolled over onto his side.

Clucking my tongue as I pretended to think about it, I nodded. "Fine. One kiss. Then I need a drink and some fun."

"And this isn't fun?" Ian asked, reaching out toward me as I moved closer.

I snorted, kneeling next to him. "Playing games to get sexual favors? Not really. If you want sex from me, you'll have to do better than that."

"But you'll let me taste you." Ian's finger crept up my inner thigh. Warmth flooded between my thighs, and I forced myself to push his hand away, lest we get stuck in there all night.

"That was different, and you know it." I cupped his face in my hands and pressed my mouth to his in a quick kiss. "There. All done. Now get up."

"Now, hold on just a second." He grabbed my hand and gave me a tiny tug. I ended up splayed across his chest and the hard-on in his pants. "I think we can do a bit better than that, don't you?"

I gave him a sassy grin but let him roll us over so that he was on top. "Fine but make it quick."

"Oh," he quipped, a fake expression of pain on his face. "You really know how to hit a guy where it hurts."

"Yeah, the ego."

"Watch your mouth."

"Make me." I shimmied beneath him, making sure to rub up against his pants.

Ian closed his eyes for a moment, savoring the sensations I was giving him before pinning my arms over my head. I arched my back, trying to get him to release me but only ended up rubbing my nipples against him. Ian captured the gasp that fell from my lips with his own, taking over my mouth like he was a starving man and the only way he would survive was inside my mouth. I stopped trying to get my arms free and instead wrapped my legs around him, grinding myself against him. Ian dropped his hands from mine and cupped my breasts, squeezing them until they ached.

I was half a second away from saying fuck the party and just have him fuck me before Ian pulled away and stood. I gaped at him, my core pulsating and my mouth swollen from his kisses. "What the hell, Ian?"

"Don't we have a party to get to?" Ian grinned, acting as if we hadn't almost fucked on the floor. If I couldn't see the form of his dick pressed against his jeans, I would have thought that whole thing hadn't affected him at all, but seeing it only made me scowl. So that's how he wanted to play it?

"Yeah, we do." I stood up, ignoring the hand Ian held out to help me. I pushed him toward the door. "I'll meet out here."

Ian only raised a brow at me, his cocky grin on his lips still. "Oh? Need to finish something?"

I knew what he was implying, but I simply shut the door in his face. Turning away from the door, I marched over to my closet and dug into the back for the dress Callie had talked me into buying recently. Tossing my jeans and tank top off, I shimmied into the form-fitting red dress that landed right below my butt. The dress was strapless, so I took my bra off. The material was thick enough that I wouldn't need it, I just wouldn't be jumping around too much tonight. I traded my tennis shoes for a pair of heels and then, with a naughty thought and a giggle, removed my panties.

"What do you think?" I grinned at Aris through the mirror. "Think it's too much?" Letting out a little pleased hum, I pretended she answered me. "Me either."

I grabbed my phone from my jeans and then frowned down at my dress. I didn't really have anywhere to put it now. With a shrug, I left it there. Not like I wasn't going to be with everyone I would want to talk to anyway.

Heading out the door, I could already hear the music filling the hallway. Only a few people were still in the halls heading toward the main corridor where the party was being held. Since this wasn't a sanctioned school event, the party stretched between several rooms in the fourth-year hallway, the majority of the people popping in and out of rooms as they mingled. I shifted from one foot to the other as eyes started to turn in my direction. Most of them were curious, others a bit lecherous, and several even waved at me. I waved back with a small smile, completely too aware of the fact that I was pantyless in a room full of people.

All of a sudden, an arm wrapped around my shoulders, and I tensed before tilting my head back to see Aidan. "Hey, sorry I'm late."

Aidan didn't smile or frown but stayed expressionless. He only gave me a two-word answer. "Stay close."

Snuggling into his side, I didn't have the strength to deny him. Maneuvering through a large group of people was easy when you had someone the size of a mountain. Most people just moved out of his way on their own but not without an interested look between the two of us. There were a few women who were looking for longer than they should, and a jealous zing zipped out of me in the girls' direction, making them jump in place. Their eyes jumped to me with a scowl until they seemed to realize who I was. With an apologetic dip of their heads, they moved to find someone else to drool over. Okay, so my family name did have its perks, but I didn't have to like it.

"Drink?"

"Huh?" I glanced away from the crowd and to Aidan, who held a plastic cup out to me. "Oh, yeah. Thank you." I started to sip it but paused at the fruity smell. "Hold on, this isn't..."

"No." Aidan's one-word answer was joined with an amused quirk of his lips.

"Well, then. Cheers." I bumped my cup against his and then took a large drink. The alcohol in it burned on the way down, settling in my stomach with a sizzle. The effects were instant. All of my nerves disappeared, and a smile slid up my lips. "Uh oh. I think I'm drunk already."

"No." Aidan took the cup from me and stroked the side of my face. "Not drunk, happy."

I started to furrow my brows but then found I couldn't, my face was stuck in a joyful expression. "Why can't I frown? I'm trying to frown." I rubbed my cheeks, shoving at them to go into position but they just jumped back up. "What did you do?" Even my accusatory tone sounded gleeful instead of annoyed.

"Helping you to relax."

"Hey, what's going on over here?" Dale appeared out of nowhere before I could happily rip Aidan a new one. Dale's eyes scanned over my form and my Joker face grin, his mouth dropping open a bit. "Uh, um. Wow. Max, you look. Um, wow."

I didn't need the alcohol to make the happy feeling coming to my chest at making the know-it-all Dale speechless. I could just imagine how he would react to knowing I didn't have anything underneath my dress.

Actually, that thought made me all too happy as well. God, my face was going to hurt after this.

"Thanks." I pulled my hair over my shoulder and played with the ends. "I wanted to try something different."

"Well, you definitely achieved that." Dale's eyes moved to Aidan and the cup in his hand. "Oh, man. Don't tell me you gave her that? No wonder she looks so weird."

I frowned or, well, tried to. Fuck, this was annoying.

"She looked stressed," Aidan confessed, lifting an apologetic shoulder. He was able to frown easily, meaning he didn't have the same thing in his glass.

Reaching up and snatching the cup from his hand, I took a tentative sip. This one didn't burn as much but did make my eyes droop considerably. Oh. Wow. I cleared my throat, the inside of my thighs rubbing together deliciously.

"And what the hell are you drinking?" Dale scoffed, grabbing the cup from my hand. "Happy Juice and Aroma Tonic? Really? So, get her happy then fuck her silly? Do you really need that much help?" The irritation in Dale's voice made me happy, and not the artificial kind.

"Yeah," I bumped Aidan on the shoulder, making my boobs jiggle hard enough that I feared they'd fall out, something the guys noticed.

"No," Aidan placed a hand on my shoulder. "To either of those things."

"Then explain yourself, because this says date rape all over it." Dale snarled, causing us to earn some attention from the surrounding students.

"You're making a scene." I poked Dale in the shoulder. "Stop it." The music changed to a slow sultry beat, and I grabbed Dale's hand. "Come on, grumpy butt. Dance with me."

Dale seemed a bit reluctant but let me lead him into an open area where other students had begun to dance. Throwing my arms around his neck, I moved my hips from side to side. Dale's hands found their way to my hips, moving along my sides. His brows furrowed before they shot up to his forehead.

"Are you...?" He dipped his head until his mouth was by my ear. "Are you not wearing underwear?"

I pushed my tongue against the back of my teeth and then grinned, shaking my head. "Nope." I let the word pop in my mouth and shimmied even closer to Dale. "I think you should probably take advantage of me before someone else does."

Dale shook his head in exasperation. "Fucking Christ, Max. What am I going to do with you?"

Arching up on my tiptoes, I slid my tongue along the shell of his ear. "You can fuck me." I let my hand trail down his back and cupped his ass. "Preferably hard and dirty."

Groaning against me, Dale stiffened and then took a deep breath and pushed me away. I frowned up at him, or tried to. The magical cocktail was still in my system.

"I can't." His shaggy hair swayed from side to side as he shook his head. "Not that I wouldn't love to, but you've been drinking and..."

"That would be wrong," I finished for him with a giggle. "You're such a good guy." I poked at his face, way too interested in the skin on his face. "Why are you such a good guy?"

Dale let out a shaky breath. "Just cursed, I guess. Come on." I lead me back to where Aidan stood. "She's completely gone."

"She overthinks everything," Aidan started, trying to reassure Dale about his choices. "I just wanted her to have fun, and I like the taste of the other one."

"That's all good and well, but a heads-up would be nice." I poked him in the chest with a stern pout. "I don't need a repeat of last time."

Dale took my hand and drew me to him. "Believe me, none of us do. Now, let's get you a real drink before you end up poisoning yourself. Word to the wise: Don't mix drinks unless you want to be flying around the campus butt-ass naked thinking you're a butterfly."

"Speaking from experience?" I giggled and let him lead me to the table with drinks.

"Not mine thankfully." Dale looked up at the ball of light hovering over my head. He poked his finger at it with a frown. "I think your guardian is broken by the way. It's supposed to warn you of dangers like this."

"She," I corrected him with a grin and then petted the air around Aris. "And she's not broken. Aris just knows Aidan had my best interests at heart." I glanced over my shoulder at Aidan, giving him a wink. Aidan smiled behind his cup. Changing the subject, I turned back to the table before me. "So, what should I drink? What about this?" I reached out and picked up a cup with a sea green color to it with a lime scent coming from inside. That was a strange combination. When neither guy objected, I lifted the cup to my mouth, but a hand jutted between it and my mouth. Frowning, I glared at the feminine hand until I found its owner. "Oh, joy."

"I wouldn't drink that if I were you." Sabrina gave me a warning look before turning that laser gaze to Dale and Aidan. "And you call yourselves her boyfriends. Really, I don't even like the girl, and I wouldn't let her drink a Leeching Pond."

"Leeching Pond?" I stared down at the contents inside the cup. "That doesn't sound good."

Plucking the cup from my hand, Sabrina handed it to a pretty girl passing by with a brilliant yet totally fake smile. "Here you go, you look like you could use this."

"But, I thought you said..." My finger followed after the girl, but Sabrina grabbed my hand and jerked me back around to the table. Picking up a different cup, she sat it in my hand with a wink. "Don't say I never did anything for you."

The new cup's contents swirled around on its own, the colors changing from blue to purple to pink and then back around again. I couldn't really tell what it smelled like. It sure as heck didn't smell like any other food I'd ever smelled. Not trusting Sabrina as far as I could throw her, I glanced at Aidan and Dale. Neither seemed bothered by the choice.

I then looked up at Aris. She didn't even flinch, just hovered uselessly above my head.

Shrugging, I lifted the cup to my mouth. "Bottoms up."

A coughing fit overcame me the instant I took a drink. Man, I thought that first one had been strong. The one might look pretty, but lava would have been cooler than its contents.

Rubbing a hand over my suddenly running nose but happy to have a clear head, I turned to Sabrina. "I don't feel any different. What's in it?"

"You don't want to know, but now you won't be able to be coerced into anything you don't want to do now." She shot a look at Dale and Aidan which really wasn't necessary but appreciated none the less. When her eyes turned back to me, she scanned over my outfit and frowned. "I thought we were making progress."

My eyes dropped to what she was looking at, and I shrugged, giving her a sheepish grin. "Sorry, it's nothing against your teachings. Just trying to prove a point." Sabrina didn't ask, but she had a humorous glint in her eyes that told me she knew exactly what I was playing at. I ducked my head to the side, searching around Sabrina who had dressed in a black dress with so many straps I would strangle myself trying to get it off. "Where are your minions tonight?"

Sabrina sniffed taking a drink of her cup. "Libby is off probably sucking face with your roommate, and Monica..." She trailed off, her eyes getting a far-off look before she straightened. A broad grin spread across her lips. "So, where are our favorite brothers at? I need their RSVP for your party."

I frowned. "But we haven't even made the guest list yet."

"Oh, don't worry, I went ahead and did that for you." She placed a hand on my shoulder, a concerned expression coming over her face. "I know how much you want to make sure the party goes well, and that means keeping the riff-raff out." Her words were for me, but her eyes were on Dale.

"What's that supposed to mean?" Dale snapped, taking a step closer to me. "I'll be at that party, no matter if I'm on the list or not."

"Right." I nodded. "What he said. And while I appreciate your help," I pulled my shoulder out of her reach, "I think I can decide for myself who I want to invite."

Sabrina didn't seem bothered by my declaration. In fact, it only seemed to amuse her further. "Oh, Maxine, didn't you know?"

"Know what?" I growled.

"Your grandmother put me in charge of everything." She giggled and shimmied her shoulders.

I gaped at her. "Why would she do that?"

A sly grin on her lips, Sabrina took a sip of her cup. "I told her you were just too stressed by finals and begged me to help. And of course, being the loving soul, I am, agreed." She patted me on the head. "You're welcome." Before I could rip her head off, she was pushing her way through the crowd and out of sight.

"You're not going to really let her take over like that, are you?" Dale asked at my side, his hand on my waist.

I look up at him and Aidan, who looked about ready to chase down Sabrina and make her take all her words back. "No, but taking it out on Sabrina won't fix anything. I'll have to take it to the source." Well, there went my happy night. Where was that Happy Juice at again?

Chapter 7

"ARE YOU SURE YOU want to stay here?" my mom asked for the millionth time. She shut the car door and stared up at the large mansion before us. "I mean, you can just as easily plan the party at our house."

Sighing dispassionately, I grabbed my bag from the back of the car. "No, not really, but I already promised grandmother I'd stay. Plus, I need to clear something up." I slung the bag over my shoulder and headed for the front door.

My mom followed closely behind me, seeming as excited as I was to be there. "You know you can change your mind at any time, right? Just because you said yes before doesn't mean you can't say no now."

I gave her a sideways look. "And you know just as well as I do, that we don't want grandmother at our house for longer than we have to. I'd like to have a house to come home to."

The reminder of what happened last Christmas when my grandparents came by for a visit made my mom shudder. Emotions ran high in our house when it came to putting the two of them in the same room. The likelihood that one of the houses would suffer was high. It was better it was theirs rather than my parents'.

"You have a point there. Hold on." My mom grabbed my shoulder and then turned her attention to Aris. "You better watch over my daughter, or I'll put you in a jar and shake you up real good."

I snickered. "You told her, mom." I adjusted the bag on my shoulder and patted her arm. I started to push the doorbell, but before I could even touch it, the door opened. It was then that I noticed the slight glimmer around the doorstep. A magical doorstep, of course. I was proud of myself for figuring it out on my own. Professor Morison would have been proud too. An older man to be in his late sixties gestured us inside.

"Ladies, the Madame is waiting for you in the salon." He wore a crisp suit of pinstripes and had a balding head of grey hair. He seemed to have kind eyes, but his face was all business, stern and unemotional.

"Charlie," my mom greeted him, not waiting for permission before enveloping the man in a hug. The butler, I was assuming, seemed to tense for a moment, not sure what to do, then hugged her back. "It's been so long. I'm sorry I haven't been by to visit."

Charlie cleared his throat, taking back on his professional look even though there was a shimmer of emotion in his eyes. "Well, it couldn't be helped. I knew you'd come back around eventually."

"You mean, Bella knew." My mom grinned and then drew me forward. "This is my daughter, Maxine."

"Ms. Maxine." Charlie nodded his head. "You are as lovely as your mother."

I grinned at the man despite myself. "It's nice to meet you."

"I used to spend all my time with Charlie and his wife, Bella," my mom explained as we moved further into the house so that Charlie could shut the door.

"Where was grandmother?" I asked, curious to hear more about my mom's childhood. She didn't talk about it... well, ever. I hadn't really realized until now how much of her former life she had hidden from me until this moment. Sure, I'd asked about it, but she'd always said she had a normal childhood, nothing too exciting. Now that I knew what normal meant for her, I knew that wasn't true at all.

"Well, your grandparents are involved with a lot of groups," my mom started, patting my arm. "They loved me, but I was never their highest priority."

"Pish posh."

Charlie, mom, and I all turned at the voice. Grandmother came gliding out of the other room, dressed in a mint green skirt suit. Stopping before us, she clasped her hands in front of her. "You were always my highest priority. Why do you think I spent all that time getting in good with the other families?"

"To feel better about yourself?" my mom supplied with a sneer.

Grandmother didn't rise to the bait. "To find you a good match of course. I never cared for the endless parties, charities, and dreary social events. Really, I did it all for my darling girl, the same way I'll do it to make sure Maxine has the future she deserves."

This time it was my turn to step in. I'd had about enough of her so-called help. "Now, about that...?"

"Charles," grandmother ignored me and addressed the butler, "please take Maxine's bag to her room and have Bella bring the tea. You know the one."

"Yes, Madame." Charlie bent slightly at the waist to grandmother before taking my bag. He hobbled up the grand staircase filling either side of the foyer.

Now that he wasn't grabbing my attention, I took a moment to look around the house. Well, if you could call it that. It was more like a museum. The Broomstein home had more of a lived-in feeling to it, and Ian and Paul's parents were never there. However, my grandmother was standing right here, but we might as well have been in a hospital with how... sterile it all felt.

The ground was an off-white, the walls an egg cream color. Even the carpet on the stairs was another shade of clinical white. The poor staff. It would be a nightmare to keep this place clean. How did she do it with kids?

"Aris, I don't think we're in Kansas anymore," I murmured to the guardian, turning in a circle.

"Come along now, Maxine," my grandmother called after me. I looked away from the foyer to see mom, and she had already moved into the salon. Preparing myself for a long boring chat that would probably involve my mom or me getting pissed off, I followed after them.

The salon wasn't any better than the foyer, I was afraid to say. However, there was a splash of color on the sofas and fireplace, slight as it was. They were vanilla colors standing out in a sea of white.

"I see you've redecorated," my mom mentioned as she took a seat on one of the loveseats. I took the seat next to her to play buffer between her and grandmother. Between the loveseat and the chair my grandmother took was a glass coffee table. The legs were white, and the entire top made of glass. I couldn't imagine keeping that thing clean. Think of all the fingerprints and coffee rings. You'd need magic just to keep it in tip-top shape.

My grandmother pursed her lips and glanced around the room as if she hadn't noticed it. "Oh, yes, about five years ago." Her eyes moved to mine, and she smiled. "I tend to change the color scheme every decade or so, keeps things lively. However, seeing as you'll be here..." She turned her head from side to side and then lifted both hands in the air with a large flourishing wave.

As if a ripple had been sent out through the house, the white coloring melted away and replacing it with a warm brown and suede scheme. The couch beneath me darkened to a chocolate brown. The coffee table morphed into something less breakable and more meant for durability. Jeez, she sure expected me to break something, not that she wasn't right.

"There, that's better." Grandmother shifted in her seat as if she had just had a Swedish massage. "You'll feel more at home now, don't you think?"

I exchanged a look with my mom and then slowly said, "Sure, if you say so."

"Of course, I do." Grandmother crossed one ankle over the other and leaned slightly forward in her seat, an intent look on her face. "So, now that we have you here, I wanted to get started on the preparations for the coming out party."

"About that..." I started again but got cut off as a plump woman with curly red hair came into the room, carrying a tray with tea.

"Oh, Bella. There you are." Grandmother didn't turn to see her but waved her hand forward. "Please, the tea. We must do a reading before we start anything."

My mom made an annoyed sound, but I didn't see the problem.

"What?" Grandmother shot a look to mom. "Do you not agree?"

Mom crossed her arms over her chest and stared at her mother. "No, I don't. I think it's outdated and simply... well... stupid."

I held back a laugh. My mother was acting, well, like me. She was usually so reasonable, but it seemed in the face of her mother, she receded to acting like a child, pouting and throwing a fit. It would be funny had it not been my future on the line.

"What's outdated?" I asked, taking the teacup Bella offered me. "Thank you."

When we all had our cups, Bella went around the room, pouring the tea. They didn't offer any cream or sugar, unfortunately, which really was the only way I would drink tea or coffee. Taking it black might put hair on your chest, but I liked mine bald thank you very much.

"Drink up now, dear," my grandmother urged before taking a drink of hers.

I glanced over at my mom to see her too drinking even though she had protested before. My lips twisted in a grimace as I took my first sip. I was about to put it back on the table with some kind of an excuse, but I saw that both my mom and my grandmother finished their cups. Not wanting to miss whatever was going on, I tossed back the rest of it, hoping that it wouldn't taste so bad if I just got it over with. Nope, still horrid. And freaking hot!

"Max," my mom placed her hand on my arm, "you shouldn't do that. You'll burn your mouth."

Letting out a small whimper, I tried to smile. "I'm fine. It wasn't that hot." Fucking liar.

Taking my word for it my grandmother sat her cup on the table, and then pointed at Aris. "I see you successfully mixed a Guardian Light potion. That's quite an accomplishment."

Jeez, everyone and their moms knew about this dang thing. I shot an eye up to Aris. "Yeah, it was pretty hard."

"But you still did it. Just like you healed the Headmaster's daughter." She smiled proudly, her hands in her lap. "Everyone is talking about it. You are making a name for yourself already, and you haven't even been in the magical community for a year yet."

"Yeah, seems like."

My mom made a disgruntled sound. I glanced over at her to see her cup in her hand, a frown marring her face. She sat her cup down on the coffee table with a scowl. "Stupid," she muttered to herself.

"What's stupid?" I reached for her cup, but grandmother grabbed it first.

Peering into the cup, my grandmother's eyes narrowed and then widened. "My dear, you really should take these warnings more seriously."

"What warnings? What's going on?" I stared down into my own cup, only seeing a pile of tea mush spread across it.

"It's stupid, superstitious nonsense." Mom sighed and leaned back against the love seat. "Don't take any heed in what she tells you."

"Why, Margaret, I'm offended. Tea leaf readings have been passed down from generation to generation. You do a disservice to your ancestors with your disbelief." My grandmother held my mother's cup out to me. "Here, take a look."

I took the cup and tried to make out what she had seen. "I don't know what I'm looking at." My lips twisted into a frown. "It just looks like mush."

"That's because that's all it is," my mom answered, grabbing the cup from my hands and setting it back on the table. "It doesn't predict the future any more than a magic eight ball can tell you what to decide."

The way mom was acting didn't make sense. There was no reason for her to be so upset over a single tea leaf reading. I mean, if it was just superstitious nonsense, then what was the harm?

"Your mother doesn't believe if it wasn't quite obvious," grandmother informed me, holding her hand and gesturing for my cup. I handed it over, a bit curious to know what it said. She peered into the cup for a few moments, her brow crinkling with concentration. "Ever since that one time, she has refused to have her leaves read again. I'm surprised she didn't kick up a fuss today."

"Would there have been any point?" My mom sighed, rubbing her forehead like she had a headache.

"Not really, but I know how you like to stray toward the dramatic."

My mom scoffed, throwing her hands up. "Me, dramatic? You should talk. All you know is drama." My mom stopped talking all of a sudden at the expression on my grandmother's face. Her eyes were intently on the contents of my cup and had all but forgotten she and my mom had been fighting. "Mother, what is it? What's the matter?"

My grandmother pursed her lips and sat the cup down. "Oh, what does it matter? It's all bull hocky like you said. Now, let's go over the party invitations. I knew you said you wanted Sabrina to choose, but I really do think it's more personal if you chose the invitations yourself."

"Hold up now," my mom interrupted before I could tell grandmother that Sabrina was a lying cow and could go die in her own filth. My mom apparently thought the cup was a lot more important now that it was her own daughter's future on the line. "You don't get to lecture me about not believing and then just turn around and dismiss the whole thing a minute later. What does it say?"

Grandmother shifted in her seat, her eyes down and the edges of her lips pulled tight. "Nothing of importance. I'm sure it's nothing to worry about."

"Well, I want to know," my mom argued, standing up to reach for the cup. My grandmother grabbed for it at the same time, and their clashing hands knocked the cup off the table. It landed on the floor, breaking into a dozen pieces as the contents of the cup spewed out. Annoyance pinched mom's face, and she snapped her fingers. The pieces picked themselves up, and the cup put itself back together again. However, the tea mush stayed on the floor.

"Oh, I wish you wouldn't snap your fingers like that. So, undignified. Only commoners need to go to such lengths." My grandmother huffed, already back to picking at my mother's faults, the cup and its message forgotten. I took a napkin from the tray and started to lean down to pick up the mess. "Oh, don't worry about that, dear. Bella will get it." As if on cue, Bella came waltzing into the room with a dustpan. She swept up the mess, then gathered the teacups and tray before leaving again without a word.

"You will tell me what was in the cup," my mom continued, staring hard at my grandmother.

"But what does it matter?" My grandmother gestured with her hand as if to wave off the incident. "You don't believe in the power of the leaves so it shouldn't be a big deal to know what it said."

"But this is my daughter. I would rather know if there is a chance for her to be in danger, even if it means believing in some silly tradition."

The look on my grandmother's face warped into a smug grin at my mom's words as if she had just gotten across the point she had been trying to make with the whole thing. My mom caught on shortly after I did, her eyes falling. She took a few deep breaths, the kind she took when practicing yoga.

"Mother, please tell me you didn't just make that whole thing up to prove something to me? Please, tell me you didn't about give me a heart attack because you wanted me to understand your side of this whole fucking tradition."

The chandelier above our heads shook with the power of my mom's rage, but that didn't surprise me as much as the curse word that had come out of her mouth. My mom just said fuck! I covered my mouth to hide the laugh, but I wasn't fast enough. A snort came out, and my eyes widened. My mom's eyes shot to me and then I couldn't help it. I threw my head back and laughed, smacking the side of the arm as I did.

"I don't see what's so funny." My grandmother sniffed. "You nearly broke my new chandelier. And what's with the vulgarity? Is that what living with the humans has taught you?"

Mom didn't pay grandmother any mind, her eyes on me the entire time. I kept laughing as I choked out, "You said fuck. I've never heard you curse before."

The edges of my mom's lips curled up and then she was laughing with me. My grandmother just sighed, clearly disappointed with us. However, we didn't let that stop us. We kept laughing until our eyes teared up, and we collapsed against each other on the couch.

"Now, if you are quite done with that, we have some work to do." My grandmother twisted her wrist, and a thick binder appeared out of nowhere. "Now, Maxine, I thought we could go with a pale pink for the invitations, maybe even a salmon? What do you think?"

Sitting up, I used one of the only spells I had mastered completely. The binder floated out of my grandmother's hands and over to me. I didn't even look at the samples, I simply shoved forth a bit of magic and set the book on fire. My mom jumped away from me, and I clapped the book shut.

"Maxine, what in the world are you doing?" My grandmother gaped at me, completely taken back by my actions.

"First off, Sabrina is a nasty bitch who will not have any say in my coming out party. This is my life, and I'm going to choose how I am presented to the magical community. And if you don't like it? I guess you can uninvite yourself because too fucking bad."

While my grandmother gasped in horror, my mom patted me on the back to cheer me on. Man, did it feel good to get that crap off my chest. Now, I only had to follow through with it. What the hell did someone do for a coming out party anyway?

Chapter 8

"YOU DID WHAT NOW?" My grandfather thankfully found me funnier than my grandmother did. By the end of our little meeting, my grandmother was ready to call the whole thing off except for the fact that my mom reminded her that she had already put out an announcement. Apparently, a Mancaster never goes back on their word. If they say there's going to be a coming out party, then there very well better be one. Sick, dying, or dead, it was happening.

"Seriously, Harold, don't encourage the girl. She was completely disrespectful. I went through all that trouble to get her samples for the party, and she went and destroyed it." My grandmother shook her head, picking up her wine glass as we ate dinner.

"You mean, Bella went through all that trouble," my grandfather corrected her, pointing his knife in her direction.

"Same difference." My grandmother waved him off. "The point is that she owes someone an apology. Now, what are we going to do for invitations?"

I speared a piece of my steak and shoved it into my mouth. "E-vites. Believe me, it's all the rage and saves trees."

My grandmother scoffed. "Trees. In my day, we didn't bother with such nonsense. You can always plant more trees, you only get one chance at a good first impression. The next thing you know, you're going to want to wear jeans and one of those awful novelty shirts."

"Actually, I was thinking more of a dress made of meat." I exchanged a smile with my grandfather as I held up another piece of steak. "I think it will really set me apart, don't you?"

"Oh, goddess, save me from this wretched child," my grandmother prayed, her eyes closed and head back. "I'm going to regret this coming out party. This is a test. I'm sure of it."

I snorted, not at all offended by her words. She was the one who wanted me to stay here not the other way around. It wasn't my fault she couldn't handle me.

My grandfather, on the other hand, was taking my presence here in strides. He lifted his glass to his mouth, amusement pulling at his lips.

"So, grandfather," I folded my arm on the table in front of me, "what exactly do you do in the magical community? Everyone is all hyped up about me being a Mancaster, but what does that really even mean?"

Grandfather opened his mouth to answer me, but before he could get a word out, grandmother steamrolled him. "I'm so glad you are finally taking an interest in your heritage." She smiled demurely, patting her lips with her napkin. "The Mancaster line is a long and prestigious lineage with family tracing all the way back to the Dark Ages."

"And yet here we sit in Atlanta, Georgia." I smirked. "Must have been some broom ride."

Grandfather chuckled, but my grandmother only rolled her eyes letting out a puff of irritation. "No one rides brooms. That has never been a thing. The same thing with the silly wand waving. Some might use them, but they are purely for show." She shifted in her seat uncomfortably. "No one in the Mancaster line would ever stoop that low."

"Except cousin Addy," grandfather pointed out, earning a glare from my grandmother.

"Yes, but she's an exception."

"Who's cousin Addy?" I asked, unable to help myself. If it's someone they didn't want to talk about, then it was definitely someone I wanted to know.

Grandmother sniffed and then let out a sigh, completely put out by my asking. "Your cousin Addy is from your grandfather's side of the family, she lives in Vegas. She runs a..." She visibly shuddered. "... magic show."

"Really?" My eyes widened, and I looked to my grandfather for confirmation.

He nodded. "Quite. She rides a broom and everything. Of course, the humans think it's all wires and such, but she was the top of her class at levitation." As if speaking of it reminded him of something, the gravy bowl on the far side of the table lifted from its place and floated toward him. It poured a generous amount on his plate before going back to its resting place. "However, Addy despises everything to do with our society and chooses to remain estranged."

"As she should," my grandmother retorted picking up her fork. However, before she could take a bite, Charlie appeared in the dining room doorway, his lips pulled into an unpleasant frown.

If I didn't know better from his encounter with my mom, I'd think he was just as stuck up as my grandmother was. However, I knew it was all a farce, or at least, my mom was enough to crumple his hard exterior, an ability I prided myself on inheriting from.

"What is it, Charles?" My grandmother shifted in her seat to meet his gaze.

Charlie shifted in place as if he didn't want to be the one to announce whatever it was he was there for.

"Come now, out with it. My food is getting cold." My grandmother waved a hand at him.

My brow furrowed. "Why does that matter? You could just do a spell and reheat it up again."

My grandmother made a face, but it was my grandfather who answered. "Magically heated food never quite tastes the same. There's an unusual chalky taste to it." He smacked his lips and took a drink of his water as if talking about it made him thirsty.

The question answered, Charlie took a moment to say, "Miss Maxine has visitors."

"I do?" I asked at the same time my grandmother asked, "She does?"

"The Broomsteins." He arched a brow, and if I hadn't been watching him, I would have missed the twinkle in his eye. "Shall I escort them to the salon?"

"Nonsense." My grandmother waved a hand and then smiled at me. "Have Bella set another place at the table. Which one has come to call?"

My lips ticked up and now I knew why Charlie was laughing. My grandmother only thought one of them had come to see me, but I bet both Ian and Paul were standing in the foyer as we spoke.

"Both of them, Madame."

It took her a moment to say anything, so long, in fact, that I thought she might have had a heart attack or went deaf, but eventually, my grandmother snapped back into herself. Almost in slow motion, she turned her head from Charlie to lock eyes with me. "Maxine, why are both Broomstein boys visiting you? Together?"

Not to be intimidated, I leaned onto my elbows and grinned. "Because I'm dating both of them."

She made a small sound of distress, and then her head jerked so fast toward grandfather that I feared it might rip off. "Harold, do something about this."

Grandfather wiped his mouth on his napkin and continued to eat his meal. "What do you expect me to do, Nina? Max is a grown woman. You can't dictate who she dates."

"Yes, I can."

"And how well did that work out for you with Margaret?" My grandmother shut up with a huff after my grandfather made his point. To me, grandfather smiled. "If dating them both makes you happy, then by all means, but they should both know that I will not take kindly to either of them hurting my granddaughter."

I beamed back at him with a giggle. "Thank you, grandfather. I'll come to greet them, Charlie, thank you." Charlie nodded, and I stood and started for the door. Pausing in the doorway, I turned back to the table. "Does this rule apply to all of my boyfriends?"

Catching him in mid-drink, my grandfather choked. Banging on his chest as he coughed, his eyes widened. "All of your boyfriends?"

I winked and left without answering his question. Humming to myself, I made my way toward the foyer. When my eyes landed on the backs of two familiar men, my eyes widened, and a small smile spread across my lips. "Ian. Paul."

At the same time, they turned to me, Paul with his boyish grin and kind eyes, one hand tucked into the pockets of his slacks as he waved a hand at me. It made a girlish part of me squeal in delight. Not that his brother didn't affect me as well. That cocky smirk of his and amused glint in his eyes could turn me into a puddle of goo on the floor at any given moment.

"Max," Ian purred, sliding his tongue along his teeth before giving me a full-on grin. "We were wondering if you would grace us with your presence."

I snort-giggled, standing between the two of them. "Of course, why wouldn't I?"

"Well," Paul reached a hand up and scratched the back of his head, "we know how strict your grandmother can be and wasn't sure if she would let you see us. You are her sole heir, you know."

Cocking my head to the side, I surveyed them. "Why would that matter? She doesn't control me."

Ian and Paul exchanged a look, and it was Ian who answered. "We figured since you are staying with her now that she might have been able to have more influence over you. And I'm not exactly the kind of person Nina Mancaster would want her daughter, let alone granddaughter, to spend time with."

I quirked a brow. "Really? It's like you two don't know me at all."

A smile tipped Paul's lips, and his eyes softened. "See, Ian? I told you, you had nothing to worry about."

"Is that what this is about?" I glanced between the two of them. "You thought I'd change because I'm staying the summer here?"

They didn't answer, but the guilty look on their faces and the way they wouldn't meet my eyes said everything.

I clucked my tongue and tapped my foot, pretending to be contrite. "I'm really disappointed in you two. I thought you were above all that. I mean, you have the same situation. Would your mother and father be happy to hear you're hanging around a human-raised witch, let alone sharing one?"

There was silence in the foyer. I paused in my tapping and peeked an eye out at them. If anything, they looked even guiltier. "They do know about me, don't they?" I slowly said, my confidence wavering.

"Know about? Yes." Paul began lifting a finger in the air. "It's hard not to know about the estranged granddaughter popping back up in the Mancasters' lives. However..."

Ian shoved Paul's shoulder and then slipped in front of him, so he was closer to me. "Forget about our parents. They don't much care what I do in any case. That ship has long since sailed."

"But they care what Paul does," I pointed out, not letting them deter me.

"They know I'm seeing you." Paul shoved his brother out of the way. "Just not that Ian is too."

My lips twisted into a frown. "What about at Valentine's? Plenty of people saw us at dinner together and kissing."

Paul shrugged. "They must have missed that gossip or are in denial."

"Either way," Ian pushed back in, "it doesn't matter how they feel about it. I want to know more about this sharing thing you mentioned."

A smirk cracked through my hard exterior, and I purred, "Oh, Paul didn't mention it?"

"No, it must have slipped my brother's mind." Ian glared over his shoulder at Paul before his eyes locked back onto mine.

Sliding a hand down my side to rest on my hip, I shifted my weight. "Well, my grandmother wanted me to invite you to dinner, but if you're not hungry... we could do something else?"

"Already ate," Ian quickly stated, followed by Paul, "Cutting back."

Stifling a giggle with my hand, I spun on my heel and started upstairs. When they didn't follow, I placed a hand on the banister and gave them a coy grin. "Are you coming?"

Not even hesitating, they scurried over each other to chase me up the stairs. I laughed and only halfheartedly ran away from them. We ran past a few curious servants, the very fact that my grandparents had servants still astounded me. However, Paul and Ian didn't seem bothered by them at all. Not surprised since they had servants themselves. Still, it put a slight falter in my step.

"What's wrong?" Paul wrapped an arm around my waist, concern replacing his eager expression.

"Nothing." I shook my head, giving him a small smile. "Come on, my room is over here." I pointed at the nearby door.

"It's the servants, isn't it?" Ian, ever the perceptive one, said as he opened the bedroom door and ushered us inside. "Does it bother you?"

Once we were behind closed doors, I tilted my head to the side. "What do you mean?"

Paul watched our exchange, not really catching on to why I would be bothered. He seemed more interested in my room than anything. It wasn't that impressive compared to his anyway, though it was still three times the size of my bedroom at my parent's house. Really, who needed all this room anyway? I could do gymnastics in here with plenty of room to spare.

"I mean," Ian took my hand and drew me over to the bed, "does it bother you that they saw us together, or is it the whole aspect of having servants that bothers you?"

I stared at him for a moment and then shook my head as I sank on to the bed with him. "I don't care if they see us, but having servants to wait on me is a bit strange." Paul took a seat on the other side of me, placing me firmly between the two of them. "I'm used to doing everything myself, but here? I can't even get my own glass of water without getting a strange look."

Ian brushed my hair away from my neck, his breath hot on my ear. "There's nothing wrong with being self-reliant. However," his tongue darted out and licked the shell of my ear, "sometimes you need to let others take care of you."

A warm hand landed on my knee, and my eyes jerked to Paul. Leaning closer to me, Paul's hand moved up my inner thigh and beneath my skirt. "I have to agree with my brother. You shouldn't worry so much. Lean on us."

Okay, so I know I teased about having them at the same time. I'd even fantasied about it. I'd even been with Ian and Aidan at the same time, but it wasn't the same. It was more exciting, more taboo because they were brothers. And now that I sat between them, Ian at my back and Paul at my front, my heart was about to pound out of my chest.

"So, what do you say?" Ian's hands slipped between my arms and sat below my chest, not touching me but teasing the line of my bra.

I chuckled nervously, turning my head toward Ian. "How did this get turned around? I thought I was the one seducing you."

A hand took hold of my chin and turned my face back toward Paul. "I thought this was what you wanted?"

My eyes darted to his lips which were so close to mine. Lids lowering, I allowed myself to be drawn to Paul's mouth. Before our lips could meet, Ian cupped my breasts and pulled me back to him.

"Don't forget about me." His mouth touched my neck. I moaned and then pushed away from him, detangling myself from their hands and standing.

"Max?" They both said my name, concern and bemusement in their gazes.

"Hold up now." I held my hands up, not allowing them to follow me. "I don't want you fighting over me. I'm not a rag doll." My hands curled into fists, I shook my head. "This isn't how I pictured it."

Ian smirked. "How did you picture it then?" He stood, one hand going to the bottom of his shirt. My eyes locked onto the skin he revealed as he pulled his shirt up and over his head, dropping it to the floor.

Not to be outdone by his brother, Paul lounged back on the bed, his fingers unbuttoning each button of his shirt. His tongue slipping out to wet his lips. "This isn't what you wanted?"

I swallowed thickly, my thoughts suddenly gone. "Well, for starters…" I paused and then a thought came to me. A slow, wicked grin curled up my lips. "I'd always imagined it'd be you two kissing each other."

Paul and Ian gaped.

I gestured at them with both hands. "Well, come on. You're the ones who wanted to make it how I imagined. Get to kissing."

They're heads slowly turned from me to each other. The look of utter disgust on their faces? Priceless.

"Now…now, hold on a second." Ian stepped back from the bed and away from his brother. "I'm alright with sharing, but that's going too far."

"Right, what he said." Paul cleared his throat, his eyes dropping to the bedspread.

This time it was my turn to have some fun. Reaching under my shirt, I unsnapped my bra and pulled it out from beneath tossing it to the ground. Their eyes watched my every movement even with what I had said hanging in the air.

"So, you're saying..." I pulled my arms behind my back, so my shirt strained against my back, and my nipples were clearly visible. "... that even if I wanted you to take me at the same time..." I dropped my arms and shimmied out of my panties. I kicked them off, letting them fall at Ian's feet. "... that would be too far?"

"Uh..." Ian's mouth fell open. They went to my panties and then to me and then jerked over to Paul before landing back on my panties once more. "Well, I don't know about that. What kind of situation are we talking about?"

Paul cleared his throat and moved to the edge of the bed. "When you say at the same time... you mean?"

My hand went to the side of my skirt, and I unzipped it, letting it hang on my hips but not dropping it. "If you won't kiss each other, how can I know what you would be alright with?"

"There are plenty of other ways we could pleasure you..." Paul started, his eyes locked on my hands as I played with the edge of my shirt.

Without an answer, I decided to stop torturing them. I whipped my shirt over my head, freeing my breasts, and their hot gazes locked onto my hardened peaks. "So just to be clear," I coyly fluttered my lashes at them, "I want both of you inside of me at the same time. Are you alright with that?" I asked, dropping my skirt at the same time.

Paul and Ian stared at me so hard I thought they might not have heard me. Then they turned their gaze from my naked form to each other. After a moment, Ian shrugged. "It's only gay if our balls touch, right?"

"I'm less worried about it being gay than incestuous." Paul made a disgusted face that made me laugh.

Climbing back onto the bed, their eyes locked on my every movement. "I'm not asking you to kiss each other." They made a sound. "Okay, so I did just do that. But I was just kidding. However," I grabbed Paul's hand and Ian who had inched closer to the bed, putting their hands on my naked body. "I do want you to fuck me. Together." I grinned up at them feeling a bit brave. "As for kissing, well, we do have two other non-relatives in our group. We can just save that for them."

Paul didn't seem too thrilled by the idea, but I already knew Ian and Aidan had shared women before it wasn't too far-fetched that they would have done stuff with each other too.

Thankfully, my words helped persuade them both onto the bed. Starting with Paul, I pressed my lips to his coaxing him to stop worrying about his brother being there and to only think about me. Ian moved up behind me, moving my hair out of the way so he could kiss my neck and shoulders. His hands moved along my heated skin, making me moan into Paul's mouth.

Pulling away from me slightly, Paul watched his brother as his fingers found the sensitive flesh between my thighs. Through partly opened lids, I held onto Paul but leaned on Ian, taking in Paul's reaction as Ian brought me pleasure. He didn't seem as offended as I thought he might. In fact, from the way his mouth parted, and his eyes darkened, I'd have guessed he was just as aroused as I was.

Tearing his gaze away from Ian, Paul cupped my breast and captured my mouth once more, a new kind of determination in his movements. A small part of me – the part that could still think coherently – did a little dance that they were going through with it. I fumbled for Paul's pants, tired of being the only one undressed, and grinned at the grunt that Paul released when I had him in my palm.

Ian made a noise and Paul glared at him over my shoulder. "Don't even say it."

Now curious, I glanced between the two of them. "What?"

"I didn't say anything." Ian smirked, but before I could ask for more, he dipped his fingers inside of me. I gasped, arching my back and no longer caring what the fuck they were talking about. My hand tightened around Paul's length at the same time, and he hissed a groan. Guess he didn't care anymore either.

It didn't take long to get Ian undressed as well, and I was poised between the two of them. Mouth wrapped around Ian's pierced length. Yep. Pierced. First time for everything, I guess. A part of me was apprehensive to see how that would feel, the other part cautious and sensitive to the other brother's feelings. Ian and my's first time should be just him and me. So, that was how Paul ended up thrusting into me from behind while I sucked his brother off.

All the working up, the teasing, the tension, made it so none of us could hold on very long. Each of us was eager for our own release. Desperate really. Especially, when there was a loud knock on my door and Charlie's voice came through the wood.

"Miss Maxine, your grandmother would like to know if you are coming back to dinner?"

I tried to pull away from Ian, but he kept his hand on my head. He shot a wicked grin at me before answering Charlie for me, "Oh, she'll be coming any minute now, I'd think."

Paul burst out laughing the moment Charlie moved away from the door, but it quickly changed to a moan when I took matters into my own hands. If anyone would be coming, it would definitely be me. Ian predicted it after all.

Chapter 9

SITTING IN MY GRANDMOTHER'S parlor a few days later, I couldn't keep the grin off my face or keep my mind off what happened between the Broomstein brothers. I was supposed to be planning my coming out party, but I was afraid I hadn't been much help. Not that my friends would be able to blame me if they had what I had running through my mind.

While Paul and Ian had seemed concerned about what would be touching what, once the clothing came off and their hands got on me, it seemed all their worries went out the window.

I wasn't exactly sure how or when the brothers decided who would do what, but suddenly, I found myself on the bed and caught between the two of them. My mouth trailed over Ian's body as fingers stroke between my thighs, turning my body into a hot ball of need.

"Max?" Ian's eyes widened and then gasped, his head falling back as I swirled my tongue around the head of him. I didn't have long to revel in my control over him before I was moaning myself.

Paul gripped my hips, while he thrust into me from behind. It wasn't the exact position I had been hoping for, but I figured we could work our way up to the real fun.

"Maxine?" A clink of dishes jerked me out of my memories, the odd sound completely out of place in the bedroom.

"Huh?" I lifted my head off my hand, meeting Callie's eyes.

Callie scowled, "You weren't listening at all were you?"

I chuckled and rubbed the back of my neck. "Sorry, what was it you were saying?"

Callie tapped the papers in her hands on the counter and shook her head. "Forget it, I can tell your mind is on something else completely. So, why don't we put the party planning to rest for now and you tell me why you have such a pleased expression on your face." Callie pointed at my face with an arched brow. "Come on, what were you thinking about?"

I blushed and ducked my head. "Oh, nothing. I swear. Did we decide on a band yet?" I tried to distract her, but I was outnumbered.

"You're not going to distract us." Trina clinked her teacup against the saucer, sitting it back on the coffee table between us. "It's clear her mind is in the gutter. See? Look how she's blushing."

I clapped my hands on my face. "No, really. It's nothing."

Callie giggled, leaning forward to point a finger at my face. "It's no wonder you're always thinking about sex. You have four guys. Four really hot guys. I don't know how you ever leave the bedroom, to be honest."

Trina snorted. "I know, I wouldn't."

I rolled my eyes, shifting to lean on the arm of the couch. "Yeah, well it's not like that. We don't just have sex."

"Oh, really?" Callie grinned, a mischievous glint in her eyes. "Then what else do you do? Compare the size of their wands? Or maybe you discuss whose stirring technique is better?"

"You really should lay off the wordplay," I groaned, smacking my head. "And for your information, I haven't had sex with all of them yet."

"What?" Callie squealed, jumping out of her seat. "How the hell have you not tapped that yet?"

Scowling, I crossed my arms. "Please don't refer to them like they are just pieces of meat for me to use as I want."

Callie flushed, sitting back in her seat. "Sorry, I didn't know you actually cared about them like that."

I opened my mouth to defend them, but Trina beat me to it. "To the outsider, it might seem like Max only wants those guys for their bodies. Even I can admit they are quite nice to look at. However, I've seen them together. It's not about sex at all."

"Though it probably doesn't hurt," Callie interjected with a sneaky smirk.

"The point is," I jumped in before Trina could answer for me again, "I like each and every one of them. And no, I don't compare them that way. They each bring something different to our relationship. I couldn't possibly choose just one."

"Well, that could be a problem," Trina mused, crossing one leg over the other as she picked her teacup up once more.

"Why's that?" Callie tilted her head to one side. "Why should she have to choose?"

Trina took a sip of her cup and blinked her big brown eyes at us. "Oh, you're really serious, aren't you?"

"Uh, duh," Callie scoffed.

I fidgeted in my seat. "I have an idea what you mean, but I can't choose. No matter what that might say about me to the rest of the magical community."

Trina sniffed. "So, you're just going to go unescorted?"

"No!" I clamped my lips shut, my brows furrowed as I thought. "I mean, I haven't decided what I'm doing yet. Can't we just figure that out when the time comes? I still have to pick a dress, the caterer, the music." I ticked them off on my fingers. "We have way too much to worry about before I have to think about who I'm going to go with."

Callie and Trina both looked like they were going to argue, but before they could, my grandmother walked in. "Ladies, good, you're together."

"What is it?" I twisted in my seat to face her.

Holding her phone in her hand, my grandmother's face scrunched into a sour expression. "I'm afraid I have some troubling news. It seems that all the caterers I had listed for you are completely booked for the day of your coming out party."

"Hmm." I rubbed my chin. "Well, that's alright. We can just use a human one, can't we?"

Trina giggled but quickly covered her mouth with her hand at my grandmother's glare.

"No, we can't just *use* a human one." She crossed one arm under her elbow, waving her phone in my direction.

"Why not?" Callie asked.

I glanced from her to my grandmother. "Yeah, why not?"

Trina made a noise, but this time she wasn't getting away from my grandmother's clutches. "Miss Morgan, why don't you explain it to her? Maybe Maxine will actually listen to you."

Letting out a huff, Trina sat her cup down. "Not only would the magical community notice the difference in food quality, but the human caterers might come across something magical. Do you really want to be worried about wiping memories during your big day?"

I scratched my face. "I guess I can see your point but still... what are we going to do for food then?"

My grandmother made an annoyed grunt. "I can place a few calls. We might be able to get someone from out of town." She turned her gaze to her phone, scrolling through the screen.

"Or..." Trina began.

All our eyes jerked over to Trina. "Or what?" I blinked.

"We know someone here whose family owns one of the best restaurants in town." Trina grinned. "And Max just so happens to be dating them."

I stared at her. "I am?"

"That's right." My grandmother beamed, tapping her phone on her hand. "I guess your brazen ways have actually paid off this time."

"Thanks, grandmother." I groaned and then turned my eyes back to Trina. "Who are you talking about?"

"The Templars, of course." My grandmother sniffed. "Aidan Templar is the sole son of the legendary Templar family. Not only are they known for their powerful seer abilities, but they make the most fantastic *Boeuf Bourguignon.*"

"I love their Chocolate Mousse." Trina smacked her lips together and rubbed her stomach. "I could live on that stuff."

I hummed, tapping my knuckle on my bottom lip. "So, you want me to ask Aidan if his family will do the catering?"

"Yes," my grandmother huffed. "I mean unless you want me to be the laughing stock of the magical community."

I suppressed the urge to roll my eyes. "Calm down. Don't be so dramatic. I'll ask him." I stood and pulled my phone out. "And if anything, we can always serve pizza, right?"

The gasp of utter horror that came from my grandmother was worth the smack on the back of the head I received in return. Wincing, I rubbed the offended spot. "I'm joking. Jeez. I thought you were supposed to be all proper and crap."

Hands on her hips, my grandmother growled, "Don't test me, young lady. Just because I'm getting older doesn't mean I won't give you a good paddling." She shoved her nose in the air and strode away, muttering under her breath about young people nowadays.

Glancing between my friends, I gave a small laugh. "So, that was fun. We'll have to do this again sometime."

"Oh no." Callie grabbed my arm as I started for the door. "You're not getting away that easily."

"What now?" I sagged, groaning. "I have a mission, remember?"

"But I want to know what you were thinking about earlier," Callie whined. "You never tell me anything about your sex life. I feel so jealous." She stomped her foot and pouted. "Trina is your roommate, but I'm your best friend. How come she knows more than me?"

Trina snorted. "Hard to not notice that much dick coming in and out of our room. My parents would have been so proud to find out I was dating four people as long as they were guys." I heard the bitter tone to her voice and gave her a sympathetic look.

Callie apparently missed it. It wasn't that surprising. Callie tended to have a one-track mind.

"Wahh, I want to be your roommate!"

I sighed. "Callie, you have a roommate, don't you?"

"Yeah, but it's not the same." Callie wrapped her arms around herself, her eyes going to the side. "Amanda is fine. Boring really. All she does is study. I'm thinking about going to Georgia State next year instead."

"What?" I gaped at her. "And give up Brown?"

Trina stood and adjusted her jersey dress. "I've got to go. If you need any more help, you have my number. I can't wait to see what you pick for your outfit. Is it okay if I bring Libby?"

"Sure. I'll see you later." I nodded, grateful that she figured out that I needed to have a talk with Callie.

When Trina was gone, I took a seat next to where Callie collapsed on the couch. "Cal," I placed my hand on hers. "Are you alright? Do you really hate Brown so much you'd go to Georgia State?"

Callie gripped my hand in hers, leaning her head against my shoulder. "No. Not really. I'm just so afraid of losing you."

"Losing me?"

"Yeah," she breathed out with a sad expression. "You've found this whole other side of you, and well, I know you don't mean to, and I know it's part of growing up, but I feel like we're drifting apart. Like you've left me behind somehow."

"Oh, Callie." I wrapped my arms around her shoulders, hugging her. "I could never leave you behind. You're not only my best friend but my sister. I couldn't get rid of you if I wanted to which will never happen, no matter how many guys I have in my bed."

"Really?" She sniffed, rubbing her nose with the back of her hand. "With all the dick in your bed, there's still room for me?"

I groaned and shoved her playfully. "Please don't say stuff like that. And no more talk about leaving Brown because you miss me, okay?"

Callie ducked her head sheepishly. "Actually, that wasn't just because of you."

My brows perked up. "Huh?"

"Yeah, I decided to come back this fall not just because of you." She let out a nervous laugh, not quite looking me in the eye. "Turns out Brown is a lot harder than I thought and so expensive. I kind of had to drop out and move back home."

"What?" I screeched, jumping to my feet. "How the... what the hell happened, Callie?"

Callie stood as well. "It's not a big deal. I flunked a few classes and lost my scholarship." She waved a hand at me as if that were enough to get me to forget it. "Besides, I'll be able to focus on school a lot more staying with my parents and not having to worry about money. Plus, I'll be near you!"

I pursed my lips. "I suppose, but I wished you'd told me before. I'm not the only one holding things back," I chastised her, puffing my cheeks up with air.

"Yeah, I know. I'm sorry." Callie hung her head in shame. It didn't last long because she perked up a second later. "So, Aidan. Which one is he again?"

I rolled my eyes. "Do you want to come with me?"

Callie pretended to think about it for a moment. "Oh hell, yeah! Wait. On second thought, maybe not. You might have to seduce him into helping, and I'm all for you having an active sex life, but I don't want to be a part of it."

Seduce Aidan, huh? I wasn't sure about that. Aidan seemed more like the kind who liked to wiggle their way into your life like a worm. He'd ended up in my bed with Ian before I knew I even wanted him to be there. I heated at the thought of seeing him again. Suddenly, the idea of seducing him into helping wasn't so impossible.

Chapter 10

IF I COULD IMAGINE what a real wizard's house would look like, it would be the Templar's home.

It sat on top of a hill with a winding driveway that crunched as I pulled through the iron and brick gate. The dark roof had a sharp pointy railing. The paneling which probably at one point had been a vibrant yellow was now faded and starting to peel. The yard was overgrown, and the wind blew through the leafless trees to make a creepy scratching noise against the windows of the house. All the house was missing was a storm cloud and some lightning for the full effect.

"Man, talk about freaky," I muttered to myself, climbing out of the car my grandmother and grandfather had forced on me. I held my phone tightly in my grip and made my way up the rickety porch. Licking my lips, I glanced back down at the text I had from Aidan.

Yep, this was the address.

Was Aidan playing some kind of trick on me? Someone had to be watching through the windows, recording me while they laughed at how stupidly petrified I looked standing here on this totally not-up-to-code porch.

Okay, so that was a bit over the top. Aidan wasn't like that. He was more the 'hold onto me while we walked through a haunted house' type, less the 'playing pranks' kind.

Scowling at my lack of courage, I glanced up at Aris who hadn't so much as shuddered. I guess if she thought it was alright then I shouldn't have anything to fear.

Yeah, right. Tell that to my knocking knees.

Mustering up what little bravery I had, I reached a shaky finger out and pushed the doorbell next to the double doors. The paint was even worse this close up, and the windows were just moments away from falling apart. From the outside, I couldn't hear the bell go off and only waited there a moment more before spinning on my heels and marching back to my car.

"Max?" Aidan's voice called to me, causing me to spin back around. The sundress I'd put on for this specific occasion wrapped around my legs and almost made me trip.

My hand landed on the hood of my car, steadying myself while my mouth gaped at Aidan's large form inside the broken-down house's doorway. "So, you do live here? It's not some trick?"

Aidan raised a concerned brown and then amusement filled his eyes, a tick pulling at the corners of his lips. "Sorry. Glamour." He waved a hand around the house's exterior. "Come."

I stared at the large hand held out to me and hesitated. He had said there was a glamour over the house. If it was this creepy outside, who knew what awaited me on the inside?

"Max," Aidan's voice deepened, and his brows furrowed, "please. Come."

Taking a deep breath in, I let it out in a rush before hurrying back over to him. I slid my hand into his, the beefy fingers curling around mine like a protective shield. I allowed him to lead me into the house, my eyes searching around us the entire time as the broken-down exterior changed into something out of *Home and Garden Magic Edition.*

To the side of the foyer, a living room set rearranged itself on its own. A broom swept and danced with a mop as the bucket of water tripped, dumping its contents at our feet.

I jumped back, and the mop hurried to clean the mess up, giving me a small kind of bow before rushing away.

"Now, this is what I call a house." I grinned at Aidan as his crystalline blue eyes watched me intently.

A flurry of short people rushed back and forth through the foyer, each of them holding something different. A tray of food. A large bouquet. Candlesticks. However, what drew my eyes to them were the pointed ears and large noses.

"Are those...?" I pointed at them, trying not to stare.

"Goblins." Aidan nodded, leading me through an opening in their hurry. "They work for my family. Better than normal ones."

I thought back to Bella and Charlie and smiled. I bet they never thought anyone would refer to them as normal servants.

"So, why the whole glamour outside?" I waved behind me where the door had creaked to shut on its own.

Aidan drew me over to a wall inside the living area and jerked his head toward the pictures filling the wall. Rows and rows of fancy awards all in golden frames covered every inch. Everything from best pie to best restaurant for the last decade or so.

"To deter unwanted guests," Aidan grunted. "Can't have a regular family dinner without them putting on a show. Everyone wants them to cook for them or caterer some big event."

Aidan's words made me wince. Crap. That's why I'd come over here for.

Sensing my distress or seeing it on my face, a poker player I was not, Aidan tipped my face toward him, brushing my hair behind my ear. "What is it?"

I squirmed in place not meeting his gaze, my teeth worrying my lip. "Well... I hate to ask, but it's kind of a magical emergency." At least that was what my grandmother had called it.

"You want my parents to cook for you?" Aidan caught on way sooner than I expected from the little amount of information I'd given him.

My eyes darted to the deep rivets in his forehead from how hard he was frowning. Shaking my head, I backed up slowly. "Never mind. My grandmother can just hire a human caterer or something. I'm sorry to bring it up." I tried to run away and forget this whole embarrassing thing, but Aidan was nimbler than his big form let on.

"Hold on," Aidan urged me back into the room, pulling me to his arms. "Tell me."

I stared hard at his t-shirt, trying to remember what character had blue skin and chased coins and not how I was going to get out of this one.

"Max." Aidan pulled me closer, his large hands wrapping around my waist. "Please talk to me."

I shook my head. "I don't want you to think I came over here to use you, especially since I know how much it bugs you."

I gestured toward the awards. Aidan hadn't said it in so many words, but I could tell by the way he glared at them. The tight downward draw of his mouth and the bitterness to his tone. There was some history there with his parents and cooking, something he would tell me when he was ready.

"Not for you, it doesn't." Aidan's finger moved in a circular movement on my waist, sending a tingle through me.

Placing my hands on his chest, I tipped my head back to meet his gaze. "To make a long story short, we have no caterer for my coming out party."

Aidan's brows furrowed. "No one will cater for the Mancasters?" The disbelief in his voice made me laugh.

"Yeah, funny, right? I guess word got around about how horribly disappointing I am as a witch." I dipped my head down, playing with the fabric of his shirt.

A low rumble vibrated through his chest. I jerked my eyes to his smiling face, almost blinded by the beauty of it. Damn, that boy could grin.

"Very well." Aidan's hand left my waist and stroked the side of my face, bringing his forehead down to mine. "If they will not have you, then I will just have to take you all for myself."

His words made my breath catch and my thighs squeeze together. "So, you'll help?"

"Consider it my gift to you."

I beamed up at him, jumping up to kiss him, but before I could let it deepen, I pulled back. "Wait, don't you need to ask your parents?"

Aidan rolled his eyes. "They would not give up a chance to show off for the Mancasters. If their schedule is full, they will clear it."

I inclined my head, still not believing how easy it had been. "Alright. Thank you again."

Aidan chuckled, taking my hand in his and leading me out of the living room. "You're most welcome, but do not think I'm doing this purely for you."

"You're not?" I cocked my head then realized he wasn't leading me to the front door but up the stairs. My eyes widened. He wanted me to have sex with him in exchange for his help? "Aidan."

"Yes?"

"I'm not having sex with you." Okay, so I knew how that sounded, but it wasn't like I was never having sex with him. Just not right now. You can't just fling that kind of stuff on a girl. I had to be warmed up to it.

"I know."

My foot fumbled on the stairs for a moment, and my eyes darted down to the ground, getting further and further away. Aidan's arm wrapped around me, helping me stay on my feet.

Glowering at him, I quipped, "What do you mean you know?" My nose wrinkled with annoyance. "Have you been having visions of me again? Do you know our whole future already?"

Aidan chuckled. "No."

He tried to help me to the top of the stairs, but I pulled on my arm, getting it out of his beefy ones. "I'm serious. It's not fair if you know everything that's going to happen between us before it happens. It's cheating." I waved a finger at him and then poked him in the chest. "That's against the rules."

"To explain for what will not be the last time, my powers do not work that way." He held a hand out to me again. "Now come, or you'll miss it."

"Miss what?"

"Just get up here."

I chased after him until we stood at the top of the stairs where a platform and railing stretched across the top of the room, allowing us to see everything below. My mouth dropped open at the sight of the goblins hurrying around the room. While I was busy gaping at them, Aidan moved in behind me, caging me against the railing with his large body.

The cedar scent of him enveloped me, and I licked my lips. I tried and failed not to be distracted by the way his hard chest felt against my back or how he brushed my hair off my neck to whisper into my ear, making my eyes close on their own.

"Watch, Max," Aidan murmured into my ear, and I forced my eyes open.

"What am I looking for?" I gasped out as his lips tugged on my ear before sucking it into his mouth.

Releasing my ear from his mouth, one of Aidan's hands moved from the banister and moved down the side of my dress. My hand clutched his, stopping him.

"Just watch," he urged me, and my hand drifted away from his and gripped the railing. My heart beat a million miles a minute as he drew the skirt of my dress up enough to slip his hand between my thighs.

I opened my mouth to protest about being in public, but it was then that what Aidan had been trying to make me see began to unfold. A goblin holding a large tower of glasses inched his way through the foyer. I caught sight of the mop on the other side just as Aidan's fingers dipped beneath my panties and slid across me. I gasped and held the railing tighter.

"He's going to fall and break all those glasses," I guessed and then let out a low moan, my eyes squeezing shut.

Aidan pumped his fingers inside of me, rocking us slightly. I could feel myself getting close to my climax, but Aidan stopped just before I could reach it. "Open your eyes, Max."

I struggled to do as he asked, my eyes opening wide as his digits moved in an even more fevered pace.

The goblin's foot found the slick spot I knew he would eventually find. His feet went up and over his head, the glasses going into the air. However, instead of crashing to the ground a glowing creature zipped into the foyer. Glowing bits moved around the room, the glasses no longer fought against gravity but floated in the air. The way the light bounced off the fairy dust and glass caused the foyer to have its very own light display. Rainbows bounced off every inch of the room and the goblins beneath it scurrying to get a big enough sheet to catch them when they fell.

A startled laugh that caused me to clench around Aiden's hand escaped me, making his movements all the sweeter. A hard bulge pressed against my back, and I knew he was holding himself back to give me this delicious mixture of pleasure and joy. His thumb flicked over my most sensitive part just as the whole glass set came crashing down, sending me with them.

Breathing heavily and leaning against the railing, I glanced over my shoulder at him. "Okay, you're allowed to see some of our future."

Aidan just laughed.

Chapter 11

STANDING ON A DAIS in the middle of a three-way mirror set up, I scowled at the fluffy monstrosity my grandmother had picked out. Not only was it pink, it was Pepto Bismol pink. Now, I wasn't one to hate on the color. I adored a baby pink or even a hot pink, but the pink of this dress made me want to vomit.

And if the color wasn't bad enough, it had enough ruffles on it that I wouldn't be surprised if a tiny dog came popping out of the skirt at any moment to complete the complete cliché of it all.

"What do you think?" I turned in a circle in the only shop my grandmother allowed me to shop in for my coming out party dress. Madame Lace was the only magical dress shop that carried the right kind of gowns, or so my grandmother said. It was named after

160

its owner, a woman in her forties with better style than the piece of crap my grandmother thought was 'just precious.'

My eyes immediately went to Callie who I knew would share my disgust. She stuck her tongue out and gave me a firm thumbs down. "That thing should be burned."

"Oh, come on." My mom smirked next to her. "It's not that bad. You should have seen what your grandmother wanted me to wear to mine." She physically shuddered in remembrance.

Thankfully, my grandmother hadn't been able to be with us, or she and my mother would have had some kind of argument. No doubt they would have gotten us kicked out of the store before their tempers blew the top off.

"Dale? Aidan?" I twisted my body around to face the chairs they had taken by the wall.

Dale had a large grin on his lips as he pushed his glasses further up his nose. "I think it looks great." I could hear the laughter in his voice, and I flipped him off.

"Aidan?" I sighed in desperation. "Please tell me that I am in no way being over dramatic and have every right to burn this thing before some other poor girl gets talked into it."

Aidan grunted, only barely looking up from his phone to look at me. It had been like that all day. Why he even bothered to come with me if he wasn't going to pay attention frustrated me to no end.

Pulling the skirt up so I could jump off the dais, I marched over to him and jerked his phone out of his hand. With it no longer in his direct vision, Aidan's eyes finally skimmed over my form, the edges of his eyes widening before they settled on my face.

"There you are," I huffed, crossing my arms over my chest. Well, I tried to. The large bow on the front hindered that act.

"What are you wearing?" He arched a brow, his hand reaching out to tug at the rows of bows and ruffles.

"Well, if you'd been paying attention," I accused, "you'd know this is my grandmother's choice. Keep it or burn it?"

"Burn it." His low, gravelly voice answered with a nod. "Definitely burn it."

"Good." I inclined my head and then started to give his phone back but then stopped, pulling it back to me. "What is so important that you've been ignoring my distress?"

Aidan frowned and then shifted in his seat. "Nothing. My apologies. Go on." He didn't even ask for his phone back but didn't meet my eyes.

"Fine," I quipped, taking his phone and tucking it in between my breasts. "Maybe now you'll pay attention to me and not your phone."

I began to stomp away, but Dale snickered. Whipping back around, the action taking more effort than usual because of the extra fabric, I narrowed my eyes on the redhead. "Did you have something to add?"

Dale balked. "Uh, no. Sorry."

"Then what's so funny?" I put my hands on my hips and gave him my best no-nonsense glower.

A small laugh followed by a movement to my left caused me to falter in my stance. Paul had appeared in the shop at some point and stood next to Callie with a bewildered expression on his face. "Wow, Max. I... uh... that's really some dress."

"Oh, you like?" I grinned, turning around in a little circle so he could see the whole get up. "I'm thinking of having you all wear matching suits."

The look of pure horror on Paul's face was worth the interruption. Before I could tell him that it was all a joke, the room erupted in laughter. Paul's shoulders sagged, and he took a seat next to Aidan.

"Don't scare me like that," he begged, pulling his phone out to frown at it as well.

"That's it," I snapped. "All phones on the table. This is supposed to be about me wearing pretty dresses and sexy lingerie." The last bit had my mom grimacing and the guys shifting eagerly in their seats. "But instead, you're all acting like some high schooler waiting for the person you like to text you back." I threw my hands in the air and then pointed at myself with a fierce scowl. "I'm here. So, who are you waiting for?"

Dale started to say something but then cried out, "Ouch. Damn it." He rubbed the back of his head, glaring at Paul and Aidan though neither one of them had moved.

Narrowing my eyes at them, I slowly wiggled my finger at them. "I'm going to get out of this dress and into the next one. By the time I come back, someone better start talking." I spun around and marched to the dressing room. "Callie, your assistance please."

Callie giggled and stood, hurrying after me while giving the guys a smug grin before I shut the door. "So, what do you think it is?"

"What?" I asked, pulling Aidan's phone out from between my boobs and tossing it on the single chair in the dressing room.

"What do you think they're hiding," Callie said over my shoulder as she worked on the laces that went up the back of the dress. Yep. You guessed it. As if I wasn't suffering enough, they had to add corset lacing up the back. Guess that was the only way they could get someone into this thing and keep it on. Though, at the moment I was pretty tempted to burn it with me inside of it. Would be totally worth it to make sure this thing never saw the light of day.

I shrugged, keeping my martyr thoughts to myself. "Who knows? They obviously don't want me to know, but I'll get it out of them."

"Oooh," Callie cooed. "Maybe they're buying you a present and want it to be a surprise?"

The back of the dress sagged, and I took in several glorious breaths of air before shoving the dress down my arms. "I doubt it. Why would they be looking at their phones like that?"

Callie lifted a shoulder. "Maybe they're having a problem with whatever they're getting you."

I rolled my eyes and picked up another one of the dresses. Callie promptly tossed the pink one out of the dressing room carelessly. This dress was more my style. While the bottom still had ball gown written all over it, at least it was more adult and less 'I'm a pretty pretty princess.'

"Wow, I love this one." Callie's eyes brightened at the white material fluttering around me. The bodice cupped my breasts, giving me a substantial amount of cleavage without showing off all the goods. It tapered at the waist before flowing into the skirt, the bodice and abdomen covered in tiny little jewels that I hoped were fake.

"Max?" my mom called from the other side of the curtain. "Your grandmother is on the phone, I'm going to step out for a moment. Don't make any decisions without me, okay?"

"You got it." I fluffed the skirt happily and turned to Callie. "Ready to see some jaws drop?"

Callie clapped her hands giddily. "They're gonna want to tear this thing from your body, you know, in a good way." She winked. I started for the door, but she put a hand up. "Hold on. Let me make sure all phones are gone."

"Good idea." I nodded. "Make sure they get the whole experience." I waited while Callie exited. There were some muffled voices and then a familiar shout that I knew was Callie's 'don't fuck with me' voice.

"Ready!" Callie called, and I pushed the curtain back and took small steps toward the dais. However, while Callie might have gotten their phones away from them, Dale was the only one paying attention to me. Aidan and Paul had their heads close together, whispering about something or another.

I cleared my throat, irritated.

The moment the guy's eyes landed on me, my skin lit up like the fourth of July. An array of emotion passed over their faces. Wonder. Awe. Arousal. Everything I ever hoped my dress would make them feel.

"This is definitely the one." I beamed, clasping my hands in front of me. I ignored the phones sitting on the floor where Callie sat and stood on the dais. I moved this way and that as I admired the dress in the three-way mirror. Pausing in my admiration, I turned to the guys. "Well?"

Dale was the first to recover. He cleared his throat and pushed his glasses up his face needlessly. "It's gorgeous. I mean, you're gorgeous."

"Thank you, Dale." I ducked my head slightly at his praise.

"You look great, Max," Paul announced, his hands rubbing up and down the length of his jean-clad legs. While his eyes were on me, I could still tell he was distracted.

Aidan didn't even grace me with a worded answer only nodded, his eyes darting to the phones.

Enough was enough.

"For the love of all that is fucking frilly," I growled and marched over to the phones. I grabbed them and tossed them at their feet. "If it's that important, just get out of here. You're ruining this whole thing by being here." I spun around not waiting for their response, my eyes burning. Freaking angry tears. Why did I have to be an angry crier?

"Max, hold on." Paul's hand landed on my shoulder, stopping me. "Please wait."

"What do you want?" I felt a small amount of pride that my voice didn't shake.

"It's not what you think." He stepped around me, not letting me hide my face from him. Brushing a thumb across my cheek to catch a stray tear, he lowered his head to mine. "We're not distracted because we want to be."

"Then what is it?" I pushed his hands away. "You're acting like it's some big secret and it's pissing me off."

I felt Aidan before I actually saw him. "It's Ian."

"What's Ian?" I twisted around to face him. I'd asked all the guys to come see me try on dresses for the coming out party, and all but

Ian had agreed to come. I actually never even got a response from him. Paul had messaged me back saying Ian had school stuff. Not too out of the ordinary. Plenty of the students did extra school stuff over the summer.

Paul scratched the back of his head. "Well, remember how he had that final he was working on before?"

I frowned. "Yeah, but school's over. He should have been done now, right?"

Aidan shook his head. "It's not so much a final as..." He tucked his hands in his pockets, looking for the right word.

"An initiation," Dale finished for him, closing our little circle out.

My brows shot to my forehead. "Initiation? Like into some kind of club?"

Shaking his head, Aidan answered, "More like a fraternity."

Dale snorted. "Call it what it is. A secret organization that only those studying the dark arts are allowed to join."

Okay, now I was getting worried. I searched out Aidan's face. "Why aren't you doing this initiation thing too then?" Aidan and Ian were both studying the dark arts though I had a feeling Ian was a bit more into it than Aidan.

Aidan's expression hardened. "The people in the group are not the kind of people I want to be associated with."

"And Ian does?" I glanced from Aidan to Paul. "Why didn't you tell me before?"

The guys exchanged a look, but it was Callie who answered.

"They didn't want to worry you, obviously." She shook her head, her brown hair swaying around her. "Four guys and they're still so overprotective of you. Man, I guess even some things can't be fixed with magic." She lounged on the couch with a 'cat that ate the canary' look.

Before I could ask more about the situation, the last people on earth I wanted to deal with came in to the shop.

"Oh, you're here." Sabrina grimaced, her eyes scanning over our group. Monica and Libby stood next to her, certainly not as put out as Sabrina looked to see us.

"Is that your dress?" Monica gushed, moving away from Sabrina and toward me, her eyes lighting up. "It's so pretty."

Libby followed Monica to my side, also cooing about the dress. For a moment, I forgot about Ian and his problems.

"Someone is missing from this group." Sabrina smirked, taking us in. "I saw your mother outside, and Libby already told me

Trina is at a birthday party for her family." Libby smiled to herself at the mention of Trina. "So, who's missing?"

Everyone was quiet. The tension in the room escalating. We all knew who was missing, and Sabrina bringing it up wasn't going to make it any better.

"Oh, I know." Libby raised her hand like she was in class. Sabrina pointed at her. "Ian's missing."

"Right." Sabrina crossed her arms over her chest and stared at me, a smug grin on her lips. "Where is our resident bad boy?"

"He had school work," I answered simply.

"Oh, you mean he's being initiated?" Sabrina corrected me.

Scowling, I shot the guys a glare, silently yelling at them for me being the last to know. I gathered my skirts and moved for the changing room, no longer in the mood to try on dresses.

Fortunately, this dress wasn't as hard to get out of. A zip and a flick and it pooled at my feet. I stripped out of the lingerie Madame Lace had insisted I wear underneath - to get the whole experience - and pulled on my regular clothes.

Marching out of the changing room, I almost ran into my mom.

"Oh, honey, there you are." My mom had her phone up, tapping on the screen rapidly. "I just got off the phone with your grandmother. It seems the band we wanted isn't going to be able to play at your party. We'll have to find someone else."

"Great." I pushed past her, grabbed my purse, and headed for the door. "I'll add it to the list." But first, I had an initiation to break up.

Chapter 12

"I DON'T NEED YOU to come with me," I told Aidan and Paul for the fifth time since we climbed into my car. "I can handle this myself."

Aidan grunted.

Paul placed his hand on top of mine. "He's my brother. I don't want him to be in this group either."

"And he's my boyfriend," I snapped back, jerking the car into park. "I'm sure you and Aidan have already run his ear off about how he shouldn't be in this secret society." I made a face and did the finger quotes. "You of all people should know no one listens to their family's advice until someone on the outside says it."

Aidan snorted, his large form filling up the whole back seat of my borrowed car.

"I wish I could say you were wrong." Paul sighed and rubbed his ear. "Look, my brother might have run to the dark arts as a way to get out from underneath our parents' thumb, but he's going to get himself hurt if he doesn't start listening to someone. I hope for all our sakes that someone is you."

I gave him a reassuring smile and patted his hand. "Me too. Now show me where this initiation thing takes place."

We climbed out of the car and made our way across the quad. Being at the school during the summer was strange. Sure, like most colleges, there were summer classes, but the absence of people made the campus feel unlived in. Creepy, really.

"This way." Aidan guided us away from the main hallways and toward a door labeled Dark Arts Department.

The door opened up to a set of stairs. The lighting in the stairway wasn't flickering or dim like some horror movie, as I expected, but had a hospital quality to them, sterile and bright.

"Aidan?" I started, holding onto the cold metal railing as we moved down the stairs. "I thought you said the basement was dark and dank. This feels more like we're going into a morgue or something else equally clinical."

Aidan tilted his head back toward me. "This is only the classroom area. The initiation takes place deeper beneath ground."

"Well," I clucked my tongue, turning slightly to Paul, "that doesn't sound fun at all."

Paul chuckled and took my hand, giving it a reassuring squeeze. "I'm here."

I squeezed back. "Thanks."

Once out of the stairway, we walked into a large concrete room. There were tables lined up like in any other kind of classroom with a board and desk in the front. However, unlike the other classes, there were several sets of doors lined up on either side of the room. Each room had a different number on it.

"What's up with the numbers?" I asked, moving away from them toward the number six door. Aidan grabbed my arm and pulled me back to his side. I stared at up at him in confusion.

"Don't go off on your own." The warning tone in his voice made my blood chill, and I nodded.

Paul kept close to us as Aidan brought us to a door at the front of the room. This one didn't have a number on it, only an infinity symbol.

"What's back there?" I whispered. "And why am I whispering?"

I had hoped Aidan would crack a smile at my joke, but his mouth was set in a hard line. It made my already frazzled nerves worse.

We stood there waiting for him to open the door, but then I realized there wasn't a door knob, only a strange golden plate on it with a sharp pin sticking out. Without warning, Aidan pressed the pad of his thumb to the pin. Blood pooled to the surface, and a click sounded somewhere. The door unlatched, opening on its own.

"Come." Aidan pushed the door further, so we could follow behind him.

I grabbed hold of the back of his t-shirt. All my wisecracks and jokes were swallowed as we stepped into a dark hallway. This was more like a Dark Arts department should look. Dim sconce lights decorated the bumpy walls. They might have been made of stone or dirt, I wouldn't have known. I wasn't taking the chance to figure it out. The magic in the air already set my hairs on end.

"Not much further," Aidan reassured me. I glanced back to check on Paul and found him with his eyes dead ahead, and they didn't dip once to look at me.

Guess I wasn't the only one freaking out.

We could hear the chanting before we even got to the doorway ahead. And when I say doorway, it was more like an archway cut out of the wall. The archway led into a circular room where a dozen hooded figures stood in a circle. The floor had a white pentagram painted on it, and in the center sat an altar. A silver chalice sat on the altar next to a couple of candles and a book.

Aidan didn't announce us to the room as he led us to stand off to the side, watching as a person stepped into the middle of the circle. They pushed back their hood, revealing the pale face beneath. A young woman a bit older than me stepped up to the altar. She picked up a knife I hadn't seen on the altar and cut her palm. Holding her hand over the chalice, she let the blood drip from her hand and into the cup. Next, she dipped her fingers into the wound and then made a squiggle in the book.

Holy crap. Aidan wasn't lying about this group being bad news. I'd only read about the dark arts, and so far, everything I'd read said that anything that used live blood or flesh was just asking for trouble. This had 'bad' written all over it.

When Ian stepped into the circle next, I couldn't stand by and say nothing. Okay, so I'm not proud of the next words that came out of my mouth. I sounded like my mother, but at least it got the job done.

"Ian Broomstein, what in the ever-loving hell do you think you are doing?" I screeched, my hands on my hips and a snarl on my face.

Ian froze.

The chanting stopped. In slow motion, every member of the circle turned toward us. The force of their eyes made me want to step back, but I forced myself to stand my ground. Hands on my hips, eyes narrowed, I locked my gaze with Ian who had sat the knife back on the altar.

He wasn't as horrified or embarrassed as I expected him to be. I knew if my mother had shown up and done something like this in front of all my friends, I'd been freaking out. Ian had balls of steel because he simply stepped over to one of the cloaked figures and then out of the circle, coming toward us.

Someone clapped on the lights, and the group dispersed to the side where there was a table I hadn't seen before filled with drinks and cookies. I guess devil worshipers had to eat too.

"What are you doing here?" Ian asked, confusion covering his face.

Crossing my arms over my chest, I poked my tongue in my cheek as I looked him up and down. "So, this is where you have been lately? Blowing people off and not returning messages? For this…" I gestured at the group of people acting as if they weren't just in the middle of some evil shit. "… whatever the hell you want to call this."

Ian ignored me and glared at Paul and Aidan. "You shouldn't have brought her here." Then his hazel eyes landed on me. "You shouldn't have come here."

"I can see that." I tapped my foot. "Wouldn't want your girlfriend getting in the way as you sell your soul for what?" I gestured wildly at the tables. "Some stale coffee and off-brand cookies, Ian? Really? What the fuck."

Ian ran a hand through his hair. "You don't understand what's going on here. Aidan, I told you I had this under control."

"You don't." Aidan had that look in his eyes like he knew something we didn't, and I could only assume he'd had one of his visions.

Sighing, Ian shook his head. "I don't care what you saw. It's not like that, I swear. They're not bad."

"What's with the blood then?" Paul interjected. "Blood has living, breathing magic in it, Ian. You know how dangerous that kind of stuff can be, and you're just going to give them yours? Just like that?"

"No, not just like that," Ian snapped at his brother. That fun-loving bad boy I was used to seeing suddenly had a sharp edge to him. "I've been preparing for this all year. Do you really think I'd agree to something like this without thinking it through?"

Paul stepped between us, so he was right in Ian's face. "I think you're so scared of our parents controlling your life that you'll sign your name off to the first person who would give you an out. That's all this is." He gestured around the room and then shoved a finger into Ian's chest. "Admit it. You're running."

"I'm not running," Ian growled, shoving Paul back from him. "I'm making a name for myself which is more than I can say for you. You might be happy to follow in our parents' footsteps, but I'm not."

I shoved myself between Ian and Paul before they could start swinging at each other. Placing one hand on each of their chests, I gave them a little push. "Alright, let's all take a breath. Paul and Aidan, why don't you let me take it from here?"

"But Max—"

I cut Paul off. "But nothing. You two interrupted my happy dress fitting day with this, and now you need to let me deal with it." I gave Paul a little shove. "Go, wait for me upstairs."

Aidan's gaze met mine for a moment. He nodded in understanding before leaving the way we came with a disgruntle Paul on his heels.

With the brother and best friend gone, I was on my own. Turning back to Ian, I sighed. "So...?" I clucked my tongue and rocked on my heels.

"You don't need to worry," Ian insisted, placing his hands on my shoulders.

"Oh? I don't?" I quirked a brow. "So, you're not about to sign your soul or whatever in that book in a very devil worshiping looking ritual?" I wiggled my fingers at the altar behind him.

Ian chuckled, shaking his head. "No. It's not like that at all. The blood is a binding oath to uphold their values and not to misuse the powers given by the collective fold."

I frowned. "Collective fold? That sounds very...cultish."

Ian drew me closer to him, his arms wrapping around my back. My hands went to the sleeves of his robe which was a lot softer than it looked. "Look, you have to trust me on this. I know what I'm doing. It's not as dangerous as my brother and Aidan are making it out to be."

I chewed on my bottom lip as he pressed his forehead to mine. "Look, I know I have no right to say anything."

"You have every right," Ian interrupted, pressing his lips to my head, melting my resolve a bit.

"I mean, we've only been dating a short while, and I am still new to the whole magic thing, so I can't even begin to understand everything that's going on here." I let him go enough to wave a hand at the room of people pretending to give us privacy. "However," my blues eyes met his hazel ones, "I don't want to see you get hurt. Can you promise me that?"

"Not to get hurt?" Ian smirked. "That might be a bit hard. Accidents do happen."

I rolled my eyes. "You know what I mean."

Ian kissed my nose. "Yes, I do. And thank you for worrying about me. I'm happy to know you care." He cupped my face and brushed his lips against mine.

I sighed into his kiss, letting him ease my worries. When we parted, Ian took my hand and led me toward the circle. "Hold on a moment, what are you—"

He grinned and winked. "Everyone, this is Max. My girlfriend."

The hooded people around us nodded and murmured their greetings. The young woman from before even came up to me and started to chat about my coming out party. While I wasn't completely put at ease about the group, I realized most of them were just like Ian, regular old students looking for a different way in life which I could respect.

However, it didn't explain the vision that Aidan had. Something told me it wouldn't be something that could be solved by cookies.

Chapter 13

LAYING ON MY BED, I stared up at the ceiling of my room. There were only a few days left until my coming out party, and everything was going according to plan.

Well. Kind of.

Trina: Did you figure out the music yet?

Me: iPod?

I waited for the inevitable ping of my phone and the snarky explanation of why I couldn't just do it the human way.

Before Trina could get her message out, my phone rang. Mom. Sitting up, I answered the phone.

"Hey, mom. What's up?" I hadn't seen my mom much since I moved in with grandmother for the summer. It was understandable since they didn't really get along, but I still missed my mom.

"Max, I'm so happy to have caught you." My mom seemed a bit out of breath, making me frown.

"Are you running? You sound weird."

Silence on the other line raised my suspicions. Then my mom came back on the phone, her voice now normal. "No, just playing a game with your dad. Uh. Twister. It's a hard game."

My brows furrowed as I tried to imagine my parents playing that game. "Why would Twister make you...?" My eyes widened, and my mouth dropped open. "Oh my god. Mom. You called me after you were having sex? Ew."

"No, don't be ridiculous." My mom let out a nervous chuckle. "We were playing Twister."

I snorted. "You're a horrible liar."

"Well, I lied to you about being a witch for eighteen years, I can't be that bad," she retorted.

Oh, yeah. There was that. Still, no one wanted to talk to their parents about their sex lives. Just. Ew. A shudder went through me as my phone vibrated under my hand. Trina finally texted me back.

"Changing the subject," I said gleefully, "what were you calling about?"

"Can't I just want to talk to my daughter?" my mom asked, her voice going up in pitch.

"Not when you just did it with my dad which, by the way, ew again." I made a face and climbed off the bed. "I hope you have something important to say that's worth traumatizing me."

My mom made a sound of disbelief. "If you're traumatized by this, how do you think your dad and I feel about knowing you're having orgies with four guys?"

My mouth fell open. "I... I'm not having orgies." I went to my bathroom and grabbed my brush, running it rapidly through my hair. "Where would you even get an idea like that? And it's totally not the same thing."

"It's worse actually. Thinking about my precious little girl getting pounded by all that wizard dick."

"Oh my god, mom!" I threw the brush down and slapped a hand on my cheek. "Are you drunk or cursed? Do not say little girl and dick in the same sentence. Ever!" Mom laughed hysterically on the other line while I tried my damndest not to vomit. "You know what, yak it up. But I'm hanging up the phone now."

"Hold on, hold on." My mom hurried to stop me through her laughter. "I did call for a reason."

"Then get to it and stop racking up the therapy bill I'm sure to have in the near future."

Clearing her throat, my mom seemed to get a hold of herself. Finally. "Since your coming out party is on your birthday, we thought it might be nice to do something with just the three of us together before. Maybe dinner? Tonight?"

I thought about it for a moment. My birthday was getting derailed by this party, and a nice, quiet family dinner would be a good change of pace from the weird, tension-filled ones with my grandparents.

"Okay, I'm in."

"Great. So, do you want to go out—"

I smacked my forehead and winced. "Actually, I forgot I have to do a final fitting for my dress today. Can I meet you somewhere?"

"Well, that's alright. We can come with you," mom replied, a smile in her voice. "Then we can go eat and maybe even see a movie?"

The hopefulness in her voice was so sweet that I couldn't help but say yes. I loved my parents, and I had missed being with them this last month or so.

"Great. Sounds like a plan."

"And you could bring one of your guys if you wanted," my mom interjected before I could hang up.

I frowned. "What do you mean just one?"

"Well," my mom drew out, "you could bring the one you picked to escort you at the party. It would be easier to get to know them one on one rather than all together."

My mom meant well, I was pretty sure. However, the fact that she thought I had picked one of the guys for my escort showed she didn't really think I'd stay with them all. She thought I liked one of them more than the other, so why bother meeting the others?

Instead of voicing my concerns, I muttered, "Uh, I'd rather it just be the three of us, if that's okay."

"No, no, of course," my mom quickly answered. "Just the three of us sounds just dandy. So, I'll pick you up to get your dress in a few hours?"

"Sounds good." I hung up the phone and tapped it against my chin. I had pushed the choice of my escort to the back of my mind, not wanting to have to deal with it until I had to, but it seemed the time had come that I would have to figure something out and soon.

My phone pinged reminding me that Trina was still waiting on my answer.

Trina: I'm not sure an iPod is the way to go.
Trina: Hello?
Me: Well, I'm up for ideas.
I sighed and stared at my reflection. The party wasn't very far off, and I thought I'd be more nervous about it. Really, I'd just like it to be over with. However, I also didn't want it to be a disappointment to my grandmother. The woman might be a big pain in the ass, but she had her moments, and I knew somewhere deep, deep down, she only wanted what was best for me.

My phone pinged.
Trina: You know, my sister is in a band.
Me: ?? Okay?
I watched the little dots telling me Trina was typing a message.
Trina: She could play at your party.
I thought about it for a moment and then typed out a message. *Me: Will my grandmother approve?*
Trina: Definitely not.
With a sly grin, I texted back. *Go for it.*
Okay, so I might not want to disappoint my grandmother, but I also didn't want to give up who I was. And that person thinks my coming out party needs something other than string instruments for entertainment.

After making a decision on the music, it was easy to go into my dress fitting without a care in the world. I was actually pretty excited. The one good thing about the coming out party was I got to dress up like a princess and have everyone dote on me. Maybe I'd find a tiara or something for my hair?

"Here we are." Madame Lace smiled, bringing the garment bag out of the back. She hung it up in the dressing room where I could get to it.

"We'll just wait here," mom told me, taking a seat back on the couch with my dad. I sat my purse next to them and practically skipped into the dressing room. I couldn't strip fast enough. I was almost salivating at the chance to put my perfect ball gown on once more.

The zipper of the bag slid down, and my eyes lit up seeing the white gauzy fabric. Then my brow furrowed. I didn't remember there being a slit there. I carefully pulled the dress from the hanger. When it fell to pieces in my hands, I let out a scream that would make a banshee wince.

"Maxine, are you alright?" my mom called out, running into the dressing room with my dad.

My dad took one look at my thong clad body and quickly spun back around and covered his eyes. "Honey? What's wrong? Did you bite your tongue again?"

"No," I snapped, and held up what was left of my gorgeous gown to my mom. My eyes welled up, and my breath came in short bursts. "My dress. It's ruined."

"Oh, I'm sure it's not that... bad." My mom's eyes widened as she took the bits of fabric from my hands. It wasn't even a dress anymore, it was just a big ball of fluff. Even the gemstone-covered top was shredded.

"What am I going to do?" I grabbed my t-shirt and pulled it over my head, shoving my legs back into my pants. "The party is in two days. I can't get a new dress made that fast."

My mom stared at the dress, blinking her eyes and not saying a word.

"Mom!" I waved a hand in front of her face, a scowl on mine. "Wake up. This is not the time to space out. And dad, I'm decent, you can turn back around."

My dad slowly twisted around, peeking through his fingers. When he saw I was indeed clothed, he sighed, then let out a small startled noise at the mess of fabric before us. "Oh, Max. I'm not sure that's what your grandmother wanted you to wear."

"No, really?" The sarcasm dripped from my words and then I shoved my way out of the changing room. Madame Lace had rushed to us at my scream and waited anxiously by the three-way mirror.

"Is there a problem?" she asked, blinking her eyes innocently.

Trying my best to give her the benefit of the doubt, I pulled on a patient smile. "Madame Lace, I think there's been a mistake. The dress in there is not the dress that I ordered."

"Whatever do you mean?" she asked, her hands fluttering around in front of her. "It is the dove white chiffon gown, isn't it?"

I cocked my head to the side. "Well, parts of it is, but it's not so much a dress as a... a tablecloth and not a good one."

Madame Lace's face paled, and she hurried to where my mom exited the dressing room, mutilated dress in hand. "Oh, my word. I... I do not know what happened. My apologies. I will issue you a full refund of course."

"I don't want a refund. I want it fixed." I shoved a hand at the dress, gathering the fabric and pushing it into her arms. "Can't you use magic or something and fix it?"

Madame Lace shook her head. "No, no. We do not use magic on our gowns. In fact, we have a spell on them so that no magic can be used. This keeps the girls from cutting corners." She frowned and lifted the dress up. Bits of it fell to the ground no longer connected. "Someone seems to have taken scissors to your dress."

"Someone as in who?" I asked, placing my hands on my hips. "Who had access to my dress, and why would they want to destroy it?"

"I don't know." Madame Lace shook her head sadly. "We have tight security here, but any number of my employees could have gotten to it. Though, I'm not sure why they would. Your grandmother is a Mancaster. They know how big of an honor it is for you to come to us for your dress."

I sighed, rubbing my forehead. "Well, do you have any other gowns that are in my size?" I gestured around the store.

"Unfortunately, no. You are quite a bit bustier than my usual clients."

I chose to ignore the dig. I have tits. Get over it.

"Can you magic me up something then?"

Madame Lace shook her head again. "No. I wish I could, but everything in the shop has the same spell on it. I cannot undo it. I cannot tell you how sorry I am."

"Not as much as I am." I spun on my heels, grabbed my shoes, and marched out of the store. My mom stayed behind while my dad followed me out.

"Hey, honey." My dad wrapped his arm around my shoulders. "Don't worry, we'll figure something out."

I jerked my shoes on with more force than necessary. "I'm not sure how. My coming out party is in two days, and since day one, it's been nothing but a big battle. If I didn't know any better, I'd think someone didn't want me to have this party."

"You might be right." My mom handed me my purse and stroked a hand down my hair. "Madame Lace is getting the security footage for the store for the last few weeks. We'll find out who sabotaged your dress."

"That's all well and good, but it doesn't help me now." I pouted, crossing my arms over my chest. "What am I going to wear?"

"Well, how about we go get something to eat, and we can think of alternatives? I'm sure there's a dress store we can find who might have your size." My mom tried to reassure me, but it wasn't working.

"I'm sorry. I'm just not in the mood to go out." I huffed. "And the likelihood of someone having the perfect sized dress for me this on such a short notice is slim to none."

"Well, then how about pizza at our house and a good sappy movie?" My mom led me to their car. "We can call your grandmother and see what she can figure something out. If anything, maybe you could wear my dress? I could spell it to fit you.”

“Didn’t you get yours from Madame Lace too?” I reminded her, making her frown.

“Oh, you’re right. I did get mine from here.” She smacked her lips and kissed me on the forehead. “Don’t worry, we’ll figure it out. I promise.”

Chapter 14

TOSSING A BREAD CRUST into the empty pizza box, I groaned. After the fiasco at Madame Lace's, mom made me go to my room while she ordered pizza and apparently back up. How she got Dale's number, I had no idea. She was a witch, so maybe they had a magical calling tree? Either way, I was happy she had called in reinforcements, though her choice in my white knight did leave me wondering.

"It's not that bad," Dale reassured me, lounging on the bed with me at my parents' house while I wallowed. "I'm sure you'll find a better dress."

I rubbed my stomach and sat up. "It's not the dress I'm worried about."

Dale placed a hand on my back, moving it up and down in a comforting movement. "What is it?"

"Too much pizza." I belched, making a face. "Ugh. I think we might be moving into that stage of our relationship where you see the unladylike side of myself."

Snickering, Dale's hand moved from my back to my shoulders, giving me a good rub. "I don't think there was any chance of me thinking you were ladylike."

"Hey!" I half-heartedly slung a hand out at him, but he laughed, taking my hand and kissing it. "I can be ladylike when I want to be."

"I'm sure you can." He went back to massaging my shoulders, and I began to forget about my overfull stomach as my head lulled forward.

"Why are you so good at this?" I moaned, letting him remove all worry from my mind.

"Too many sisters whose only weakness was a good neck massage." Dale chuckled, pausing for a moment to press his lips to the side of my neck. "Sisters can be very vicious when they want to be. It's good to know exactly," his hands slipped from my shoulders to my back, "what buttons," they slipped between my arms to cup my breasts, giving them a good squeeze, "to press."

Leaning back against him, I let him fondle me for a moment. When his fondling became more of a seduction, I wiggled against him in search of the evidence of his arousal.

"Why, Mr. Varens," I cooed, palming him through his jeans, "is that a wand in your pocket or are you just happy to see me?"

Dale snort-laughed and even I cracked up at the hilarity of what I had just said.

"Okay, even I admit that was corny." I wiped my eyes and sat up just as my phone pinged.

Paul: Sorry about your dress. Wish I could be there.

"Seems like word travels fast," Dale said, reading over my shoulder.

I shrugged. "If he's still with Aidan trying to talk Ian out of joining that secret society thing, it's more likely that Aidan had a vision."

Dale nodded in understanding. "It is helpful in times like these. I only wish there was more I could do. Sadly, I lack the resources the others have to fix all your problems."

Trying to lighten the bitterness in his tone, I grabbed his face and kissed him so hard that even I had a challenging time breathing when we finished. "Don't forget, you have other great qualities too."

"Like what?" he breathed against my mouth. "You just want me for my body."

"And the others for their money and power," I teased back and then became more serious. "No, really, Dale. There's so much more to you... all of you than what you think. I know it might seem like I'm just being selfish keeping you all to myself, but I really do care about each and every one of you."

"I know," Dale said softly, "and you're just as hard on yourself as I am. This party, for example. You're doing it to please your grandmother though you couldn't care less about fitting into their social circle."

I lifted a shoulder and dropped it. "The things we do for family. I just wished things were going a bit easier than it has been. I wouldn't have agreed if I'd known it was going to be one dramatic issue after the other."

"Maybe this is a sign?"

"A sign of what?" I scowled, kicking the comforter further down the bed as if it were the thing that had offended me.

Dale shifted closer to me, wrapping an arm around my shoulders. "A sign that maybe you shouldn't be having a coming out party. I didn't have one, and I turned out fine."

I moved my head from his shoulders briefly to stare up at him. "That's what you think."

"What?" Dale gaped. "What's wrong with me?"

I snorted and placed my head back on his shoulder. "Nothing. You're perfect." To myself, I muttered, "A perfect pain in the ass."

"I heard that."

"You were meant to," I shot back, giving him a cheeky grin.

"You know, I'm only going to let you get away with that cheat shot because you're upset and need someone to lash out at." He kissed my forehead, and my eyes fluttered closed. "However..." Without warning, his fingers tangled in my hair and pulled my head backward. Not enough to hurt but enough that I could feel his strength. My wide eyes locked with Dale's. A serious glint that made me shiver reflected through his glasses. "Don't think that talking to me that way won't get you a red bottom in the future."

I swallowed thickly and tried to nod but couldn't because of Dale's hold on my head. Seeing my dilemma, Dale released my hair and smoothed a hand down the back of it before kissing me on the nose as if nothing happened.

Staring up at him in awe and, if I admitted it to myself, arousal, I fiddled with the material of my pants. "So…" My mouth formed a prominent o drawing his attention to my mouth. "You'd really spank me?"

Pushing his black-rimmed glasses up the bridge of his nose, Dale smirked at me. "You bet your sweet ass I would."

Licking my lips, I squirmed in my seat, highly tempted to test him on that threat. I opened my mouth to say something really naughty, I was sure, but my mom came through the bedroom door before I could use my feminine wiles.

"Hey, Max." She peeked her head around the door. When she seemed pleased by what she saw, she pushed the door completely open. "So, I talked to your grandmother."

I sniffed and grinned. "You mean, argued with." I glanced up at Aris, tempted to put my hand up and see if she would high five it. Dale squeezed my side, reminding me my mom was still talking.

"We weren't arguing. We were just trying to figure out the best way to get you a new dress." Mom sat on the edge of my bed, her eyes darted down to our entangled legs but didn't say anything.

"Did you find someone to make me a dress?" I moved out of Dale's embrace and eagerly shifted toward her.

An unreadable expression crossed my mom's face, and she forced a smile. "Well, no. Not yet. It seems all the shops in Atlanta have been bought out."

"Bought out?" My tone raised to an almost glass-breaking pitch. "How does a store just run out of dresses? That's what they sell."

My mom shrugged. "There are over a hundred ladies coming to your coming out party, many of them with enough money to do just that. They probably wanted options."

"But now they've ruined my whole party because they needed options," I snarled. Dale tried to pat my back in comfort, but I pushed away from his hands and off the bed. "What are we going to do now? I can't show up to my own party in jeans and a t-shirt." I crossed my arms over my chest and paced the room, not paying any mind to the way Dale and mom stared at me.

Mom stood and went to my closet. "Well, what if we took one of the dresses you already have?" She grabbed the pale blue dress I'd worn to my graduation last year and laid it across my bed. "We could magic it into a ball gown."

I narrowed my eyes at the dress, not quite believing my mom had the skills for that. "Have you ever made a dress before?"

Shrugging, mom gave me a reassuring smile. "How hard can it be? I'll look up something online as a reference as to what to make and then wham-bam, thank you, ma'am. You have a dress fit for the party."

I covered my mouth, giggling. "Mom, no one says that anymore."

"I just did, so they do." She picked up the dress and winked. "Now, I'm going to work on your dress. It might take me a while, but you should get some sleep." She gave a pointed look at Dale before shutting the door behind her.

Dale shifted off the bed. "I guess I should go."

"What? Why?" I climbed back onto the bed holding a hand out to him. "But I'm not done being cheered up yet."

Dale chuckled. "I think your mom has it under control, and she looked like she wanted me to leave."

"Well, I don't want you to leave. Doesn't that count for anything?" I pouted.

Dale leaned down and nipped my lip, making me grin. "Fine, but if your mother decides I'm a bad influence, I'm blaming you."

I giggled and pulled him onto the bed with me. "Yes, sir."

Dale growled, "Say it again."

I peered up at him innocently. "Yes, sir."

Dale tackled me to the bed. I let out a squeal. "Shh." Dale hovered over me, his fingers pressing to my mouth. "Do you want your parents to hear us?"

Without telling him, I gathered my magic and pushed it out around us, firmly placing us in a cone of silence. "There. Fixed."

Dale quirked a brow. "You do realize she probably felt that and now knows I'm up here deflowering her daughter."

I grinned brightly. "Oh, believe me, she knows. She thinks we're all having orgies."

Dale made a choking sound. "Orgies?"

I angled my head up and licked his nose. "Yep. You're now part of my devious harem. So, since we're all going to hell anyway," I slid my hand between us, grasping him firmly in my grip, "we might as well go down the right way." I pulled the zipper of his pants slowly down, releasing him from his pants.

Dale groaned but didn't protest. "Max. I'm supposed to be making you feel better."

I smirked devilishly, giving him an extra tug, enjoying the way he thrust into my palm. "Feels good to me."

"You're going to be the death of me," Dale growled, grabbing my hands and pinning them above my head.

"As long as you die with my name on your lips." I murmured before his mouth captured mine. Our tongues tangled together as Dale worked on fulfilling his promise to make me feel better.

Shifting so he could hold my hands with one hand, he cupped my breast with his free one. I arched into his palm, rubbing my hardened nipple against it. I growled into our kiss when my bra hindered his touch.

Chuckling, Dale released my lips for a millisecond, the air stiffened, and then Dale's hand was touching my bare skin.

Through our kiss, I muttered, "You better not have destroyed that bra. It was my favorite."

Dale grinned against my mouth. "It's on the floor." The hand on my hands let go, but I found my arms stuck in place. A small thrill ran through me. I was completely at his mercy. Raising a brow, Dale smirked. "Now, what was it you said about going down together?"

I only had a second to giggle before Dale treated the rest of my clothes to his magical treatment. My legs spread wide, Dale settled between them, not giving me a moment to focus on what he was doing before making me cry out.

"Ah. Dale." I pinched my eyes closed, focusing on each movement of his mouth, each swirl of his tongue, before he had me careening into the abyss.

My chest heaving, my eyes fluttered open to lock with Dale's smug ones. I tried to pull at my arms, but they were still spelled into place. Dale quirked a brow, and then suddenly I was free.

"Wish I had that much power in my eye brow." I retorted, earning me a dark chuckle. With a cheeky grin, I reached for him. "My turn." However, before I could return the favor, the window burst open.

In flew what looked like a drag queen riding a broomstick, her arms opened wide and a big grin on her made-up lips. "Dry those tears, my dear, because cousin Addy is here."

Chapter 15

"OH, MY, IT LOOKS like I'm a bit too late. Someone else has already put a smile on that face." Addy grinned largely, turning slightly to the side as Dale and I scrambled for our clothing.

Once fully clothed, I went to the bedroom door, opening it, and shouted, "Mom! Cousin Addy just flew into my window."

"Cousin Addy?" mom shouted back, surprise coloring her voice. "From Vegas?"

I glanced back at the bright purple sequin dress covering Addy's voluptuous form. Her blonde hair was piled up so high on her head that it had to either be a wig or magic keeping it in place.

Smirking at Dale's blushing face, I yelled in return, "I'd say so."

"No need to shout. I'm right here." My mom appeared at the door, and I moved out of the way for her to come in. Dad followed after her to my surprise.

His brows shot up to his forehead when he took in the poised form of cousin Addy doing her best to bat her long fake lashes at Dale. "That is cousin Addy?"

I smirked. "So I've been told."

My mom wasn't weirded out at all by this six-foot-something woman standing in the middle of my room as if she had just come off the Vegas stage. "Addy, I didn't think you were coming. When did you get in?"

Addy held her broom out with a smug smile. "Just now."

"Still playing the broom flying witch gig, huh?" My mom hugged her tightly, oblivious to the rest of us.

Addy embraced her like a long-lost child, her eyes moving from my mom's head to my father. "And I see you are still playing the human card."

"Addy," my mom warned, pushing away from her. Adjusting her clothing, well, more like brushing off the excess glitter from Addy's clothing, mom turned to the rest of us. "This is my husband, Wesley." She and dad wrapped their arms around each other, looking the very picture of domestic bliss.

"Well," Addy pushed up her breasts and pouted her lips, "I'm very happy for you." Her large blinking eyes landed on me. "And I've already met your daughter, Max." She winked. "A bit more than I expected this early in the relationship actually."

I flushed down to my toes. "Well, I'm not the one who just burst into someone else's room unannounced."

"And if you had been going to sleep and not messing around, you wouldn't have had this embarrassment to relive." My mom wagged a finger at me and then gestured to Dale who hadn't stopped blushing since Addy came swooping in. "Look what you did to poor Dale. He's traumatized. You'll be lucky if he ever gives us grandbabies now."

If possible, Dale looked even more horrified.

Unable to help myself, I poked at his side. "That's alright. He's still pretty good with his hands, and I have three others." Dale swatted my butt behind my parents' back, reminding me of his warning of a spanking.

"Oh, Max," my dad groaned, rubbing his face. "Now, I need to bleach my ears out."

Cousin Addy, however, took it all in stride. "I had heard a rumor that my new cousin was more my kind of person." She scanned me up and down with a hopeful glint in her eyes.

I giggled. "If they come with your fashion sense, I'd love to be part of your people." I gestured to her outfit. It made me hugely aware of my lack of fabulousness.

"Don't mind, Max." My mom wrinkled her nose at me. "She's still sour over the fact that she has yet to find a new dress for her coming out party. You are coming, right?"

"Why else would I lower myself to come back to Atlanta of all places?" Addy's face scrunched up in distaste. "I heard my new cousin was a fierce and fabulous breath of fresh air and had to come to see for myself."

I beamed back at her. "Well, here I am. Fresh air and all." I opened my arms to my sides, shifting from side to side.

Addy leaned her broom against the end of my bed and circled around me. Dale moved out of her way so she could take me in completely, or maybe he was too embarrassed by having been caught with his dick out to go near her.

"Not bad," Addy commented after a moment, tapping her chin. "You could use a bit of blush, but I can work with it." She laced her fingers and cracked the knuckles. "Let's get started."

My eyes going wide, I held my hands up. "Hold on a second. Get started with what?" I glanced around the room at everyone else seeing if they knew what she was talking about.

"You said you needed a dress, Max." My mom gestured to cousin Addy. "This is your answer."

Arching a brow, I turned back to the sequined beauty. "You can make me a dress? What are you, my fairy godmother?"

Addy threw her head back and laughed. "Oh, no, honey. A fairy I might be, but I have way more of a magical kick than any old godmother would." Reaching between her cleavage, she pulled a long stick out with a shiny purple ball on the end. Was that a wand? Before I could ask, she twirled the stick in the air. "Go on, give us a spin. Can't expect me to do all the work."

Frowning my disbelief, I held my hands out to my sides and slowly turned in a circle. The air in the room thickened and sparkled before my eyes. Purple and pink glitter gleamed all around me, and I sneezed.

Normally, I would have been apprehensive about letting someone I didn't know do a spell on me. I barely let myself do spells on me. However, my mom seemed to trust her, and Aris wasn't freaking out, so I figured I was safe enough.

"Oh, Addy, still so over dramatic with your magic," my mom huffed from somewhere in the room. I couldn't see past the cloud of sparkles and was half afraid to move in case I ended up with my head on my ass.

"You know, Peggy, I remember you liking my dramatics when I helped you with your wedding dress," Addy's voiced crooned out through the fog.

Mom got help from Addy? I grinned. Oh, she was so going to hear about this.

"Now, don't move, dearie, I haven't done a Cinderella since your mother." She stopped and then snorted. "Well, not the magical kind anyway, but that's a story for another time."

When the magic touched my skin, making it itch, I couldn't stay silent any longer. "Uh, Addy?"

"Yes, dear?"

"Is it supposed to be so itchy?" I wiggled my fingers trying my best not to scratch, my eyes squeezed tightly shut. "And can I stop spinning yet?"

"Oh, yeah. Sorry about that. The spinning is just to make sure I get all of you." She cleared her throat, and I could feel her move in closer. "Now, what was that spell?"

"Bibbidi Bobbidi Boo?" I offered up with a lift of my shoulder.

"Pfft. The writer of that one was on some good ganja. Freaking pumpkins into carriages. Mice and lizards? Those poor creatures." I cleared my throat interrupting her rant. "Yes, sorry, hon. Here we go."

I peeked out into the cloud, bracing myself for the sparkles to get in my eyes. However, when it seemed safe, I opened them fully. Addy waved her wand in the air in a figure eight motion directly in front of me. The glittery smoke spun around me, swirling and whirling until it resembled that of a tornado. My hair lifted up in the air around me, and my eyes widened. Bracing myself to be lifted off the ground, I was surprised and happy to see my feet stayed firmly in place.

I couldn't say the same thing about my clothes, though. The fabric of my jeans split at the seams, moving and elongating into a skirt. Layer sprouted from within the fabric shimmering blue and purple just like the magic around me.

My shirt went next. I had half a second to remember I really liked this shirt before it split down the middle, warping itself into something completely different. The sleeves wrapped around my upper arms, slimming and turning sheer to match the skirt. The torso of it latched onto my chest, molding into a form-fitting top before latching onto the skirt at my waist.

If I had ever dreamed of a fairy godmother moment, this would have been it, but even better. The dress I had chosen at Madame Lace's had been nice. Great even. But this one, this was better. It was a dream that glided across the floor as I moved and shifted, taking in my new gown.

"Oh, Addy," my mom clasped her hands together gushing. "You have out done yourself."

I beamed at my mom, giggling with her as I spun around. Addy blew on the tip of her wand with a toothy grin. "I know."

Releasing my mom's hands, I went to Dale. "What do you think?"

Dale's eyes skimmed my form, his brows shooting up high into his hairline. "I have to say..." He shook his head slowly and then wiped a hand over his mouth. "Wow. I mean, I've never been into the whole dress up thing, but I think I could be converted."

Laughing at his gawking, I pressed my mouth against his with a loud smack. I practically danced away from him and across the room over to where Addy stood. "Addy, this is so great. I can't thank you enough." I wrapped my arms around her with a grin so big it made my cheeks hurt.

"Well," Addy laughed, hugging me in return, "you can thank me by letting me do your hair and makeup. It'll be just the punch in the face your grandmother needs." She winked at me.

"You got it." I gave her a thumbs up and then paused. "Uh, you're not going to..." I gestured at her own made-up face, not knowing how not to be rude about what I wanted to say.

"Don't worry." She grinned, brushing my hair off my bare shoulder. "You will look fabulous, not Vegas fabulous but everyone will be talking about your coming out party for years to come. I promise."

My smile cracked slightly, but I forced myself to relax. Everything was coming together, and I wouldn't let myself stress for one more minute. After all, I had the whole party to do that. My grandmother would see to it.

"So," cousin Addy clapped her hands together, "where can a girl get a drink around here? I'm parched."

"Right this way." My mom ushered Addy out of my room and down the stairs. My dad grinned and winked at me before following them out.

I could hear him asking Addy, in his unembarrassed way, "So, Addy... does that stand for Adam or...?"

"Wesley!" my mom's voice boomed up the stairs.

Closing the door behind them, I twisted back around to Dale. Hands behind my back, I swished my skirt from side to side. I couldn't get enough of the dress. It had to be the most gorgeous thing I'd ever own.

"Are you ever going to take that thing off?" Dale's lip ticked up at the edges, and his eyes beamed with laughter.

"Yeah." I tucked my tongue between my teeth. "When you take it off me." I sauntered over to him, so I stood between his thighs.

"Really? After your cousin just caught us?" Dale chuckled, his hands holding my waist. While his mouth might be saying no, I could feel the front of him more than happy to oblige me.

Lacing my hands behind his neck, I dipped my face down to his, nipping at his lips. "While I would love to continue where we left off, I doubt we are that lucky."

"Oh, I think we could make our own luck," Dale teased, his hands cupping my ass through the dress. However, before he could capture my mouth, I pulled back.

Dale's brows furrowed.

"No, seriously. I can't get this thing off on my own. I don't even know if there's a zipper."

"Oh." Dale pursed his lips, pushing his glasses up his nose. "Well, turn around."

216

I did as he asked, a bit worried I'd have to ruin the dress just to get it off. If that were the case, I'd just wear it until the party was over. Sleeping might be a problem, but I'd stay awake for two days if I had to.

"Ah, here it is." Dale's nimble fingers pulled on something and the back of the dress loosened before falling forward. I hadn't found my bra in that scramble and was very aware of it when the dress was hanging off me.

"Thanks," I breathed.

"No problem," Dale murmured, his fingertips trailing down my spine making my breath hitch.

"You should probably head home." My mouth might be telling Dale it was time to go, but my body leaned into his touch, aching for more.

"That would probably be a good idea." Dale's mouth brushed my ear. One hand slipped into the top of my dress, and I released it as he found my breast, the dress pooling at my feet. I spread my legs, ready for the other hand that was inching down my stomach.

"The silencing spell is still on," I reminded him, letting out a breathy moan. "We could still... maybe." I gasped and reached a hand back to grab onto his hair.

Unfortunately, just as Dale's fingers sunk into me, my mom called back up the stairs, "Maxine, get down here. I'm making hot chocolate."

"Ignore her, and she'll leave us alone," I told Dale, pushing onto his hand.

"Are you sure?" Dale urged me toward the door. I stepped out of the dress and braced my hands against the wood. I pushed against him, rising up on my toes to get more friction.

Dale's hand left my core, and I groaned in frustration. I opened my mouth to protest, but something even better replaced his hand. My hands grabbed for something to hold onto, but only found one of my jackets hanging up on the door. I held onto it for dear life as Dale thrust into me at a rapid pace. I squeezed my eyes closed and pushed my hips back, taking him deeper.

My head jerked back from the door, where Dale's hand grabbed my hair, arching my neck so I could see him out of the corner of my eye. "You like this don't you?" He growled in my ear but didn't give me a chance to answer. "You like me fucking you while your family waits downstairs with hot chocolate. And. Marshmallows." Each word he paired with a thrust of his hips, making me cry out.

"Yes," I bit out, my teeth grinding. "Please."

Giving me what I wanted, Dale released my hair and took me by the hips. In an almost abusing pace that left me gasping and wanting more, Dale took me against the door, my family just within hearing distance.

It only took moments before I was clenching around him, struggling for something to hold onto as I peaked. Dale released my hips, no doubt leaving bruise marks on my skin. Not that I was complaining. He kissed my shoulder and brushed my hair away from my face.

"How's that for lucky?" he asked.

I giggled and then groaned. Ugh. I was going to feel this in the morning.

I barely moved away from the door before a banging on it startled us both.

"Just so you know, only the room is silenced not the door," my dad's voice announced through the door, followed by my mom and cousin Addy's laughter.

Oh, God. Kill me now.

Chapter 16

THE NIGHT BEFORE MY coming out party, I spent the day in the library. I needed something to keep my mind off the coming party, and a dirty romance was exactly what I was in the mood for.

I found exactly what I was looking for, reading about this main heroine, Kat, as she tried to decide between the two main guys, one a broody prince and the other a devilish shifter. With my own romance scenario ongoing, I couldn't help but wonder why she had to choose. Two was always more fun than one.

Speaking of more fun, I rolled my eyes up at Aris as I pulled out my phone. "Don't judge me." I started to scroll through my contacts when a throat cleared.

"Miss Maxine." Charlie appeared in the library door. "You have a visitor."

Ian appeared in the doorway behind Charlie, his hands in his pockets and looking as delectable as ever. "Man, I thought my parents had a lot of books."

I smiled from my seat in the library. "What are you doing here?" I threw my legs over the chair, planting my feet on the floor. I met him in the middle of the room, my arms going around his neck.

"I thought you might need some cheering up." He brushed his nose against mine, his lips snipping at mine. "I heard about your dress. I'm sorry." Ian's hand slid up my waist and cupped my shoulders pulling me closer. "Is there anything I can do to make you feel better? Maybe in the clothing optional category?"

I threw my head back and laughed. "Well, I don't think my grandmother would be too happy if I defiled her library." I skimmed my eyes over the room, unable to help how my eyes landed on several potential surfaces Ian and I could get naked on. I still hadn't forgotten about the piercing in Ian's pants. My eyes dipped to the zipper of his pants and I was tempted. Oh, so tempted.

"Well, that's what beds are for..." Ian drew out, but before I could contemplate those thoughts, he smirked. "However, I think I have something else in mind. Sadly, it requires clothes.”

Smiling, I cocked my head to the side. “Oh? Really? And what’s that?”

“Well,” Ian released me, taking my hand and leading me out of the library, “I figured since you already had a new dress, the only thing I could offer you is a little revenge.”

“Revenge?”

Ian led me to the front door, opening it to reveal his motorcycle. “What do you say? Want to go for a ride?” The way he said it made it clear he was talking about more than just the motorcycle.

“Sure, give me a second.” I held a finger up and released his hand. Running up the stairs, I ran to my room and grabbed my shoes. On the way back to the front, I came across my grandfather.

“Oh, good. I was meaning to talk to you.” My grandfather took his glasses off and gestured with them as he spoke. “This whole incident with your dress, and the catering—”

“And the music,” I reminded him with a grimace.

“Yes.” He inclined his head. “I hate to even bring this up, but I feel as if maybe someone does not want you to have this party. Can you think of anyone who would want that?”

I almost blurted out Sabrina but then stopped myself. Pressing my lips closed, I shook my head. "Nope. No one."

"Hmm. Well, I'll think on it. Your grandmother and I do have our fair share of enemies, but none that would care so much about something like this." His eyes glazed over obviously in thought.

"Alright," I drew out, my head turning toward the stairs. "Well, I have to get going. Ian's taking me out."

"Oh, yes. Yes. Of course." He nodded, waving me off. "Have a good time. Don't stay out too late. Don't want you dragging your feet tomorrow."

"I won't and thanks." I darted past him and down the stairs before my grandmother or anyone else could stop me. Grinning like a fiend, I accepted the motorcycle helmet Ian offered me and threw my leg over his bike. "So, where to?"

Revving the engine, Ian smirked over his shoulder. "How about a little breaking and entering?"

I stared at his back, a surprised laugh coming out.

I held on tight, enjoying the feel of the motorcycle between my thighs and Ian's delicious abs beneath my fingers. There's a reason guys with motorcycles are called bad boys. All that vibration and touching? It'd make a nun frisky.

By the time we arrived at our destination, I was more than ready to do that clothing optional thing Ian had suggested before. That was until I saw where we were. Madame Lace's.

"What are we doing here?" I asked, climbing off the bike. I handed the helmet over to Ian and he turned off the bike.

Ian ran a hand through his hair, making it fall effortlessly back into place. I bet he used magic to get such perfect hair. "I thought you might want to find out who destroyed your dress."

My lower lip pushed out, my brows scrunching together. "How are we going to do that? My mom told me Madame Lace outsources her security and it would take a day or so to get the evidence we need."

Giving me a sly wink, Ian grabbed my hand and pulled me toward the building. "That's the beauty of being a wizard."

I snickered and let him bring me to the side door of the building where a door reading *Staff Only* stood. "So, do you know how to pick a lock?"

Ian rolled his eyes. "Humans."

"Hey," I poked him in the rib, "I resent that. My best friend is a human and I can't help it if I don't know. Just use a spell or whatever before we get caught."

I eyeballed the empty parking lot, expecting someone to jump out at us at any moment yelling, "Gotcha." Aris didn't seem bothered, but that wasn't really a relief. That ball of light was about as useless as a g-string.

"Aren't there like alarm spells for this kind of thing?" I gestured at the building.

Ian glanced over his shoulder from where he stared at the lock. "Yes, which is why I need to concentrate. Shush."

I pursed my lips, crossing my arms over my chest as I watched him. After a few moments, I got tired of waiting. "Are you done yet?"

"Shh." He held a hand up the universal sign to be quiet and then, not a second later, cursed. "Fuck."

"Can't break it?" I asked, raising a brow. "I thought you were in the Dark Arts program. Isn't that all about doing crap like this?"

Ian stood. "No, it's not. It has nothing to do with breaking locks or laws or any of the stuff you think it is. Regardless, I'd be able to break this spell if I had the right tools."

"I thought you didn't need to pick it?" I couldn't help the smug grin on my lips.

"I wouldn't normally, but it seems Madame Lace is a bit more paranoid than the average witch." He scratched the back of his head. "She locked the door with an anti-thief spell and normal locks. I can't magic it open with a simple spell. It has to be unlocked and dispelled at the same time."

I frowned, my eyes scanning around the door and landing on a very obvious rock on the ground next to an empty coffee tin being used as an ash tray. I grinned, moving toward it.

"No way," I muttered to myself. Picking the rock up, I turned it over. I found the latch to the bottom of the hide-a-key and pushed it open. Pulling the key out, I turned back around and held it up. "How much you want to bet this goes to that door?"

Shaking his head in disbelief, Ian inched back over to the door with me. "Okay, so I have to do the spell at the same time you turn the key. We have to be perfectly in sync or we'll set off the alarm."

Taking a deep breath, I shifted into position. Sliding the key in, Ian stood behind me, his body heat on my back as he prepared to do the spell. His mouth sat at my ear, his hot breath on my skin. "Feel for magic."

As soon as he said the words, I could feel the tell-tale sign of magic, brushing my skin and running down my arms. It took a quick detour to caress my inner thigh, making me giggle before moving down my arm and into the hand holding the key.

Just before he spoke, I felt the magic slip out of my hand. "Now." I turned the key and held my breath half expecting the alarm to sound but all that I heard was the door lock clicking.

"See? We make a great team."

We pushed the door open and quietly snuck inside the building. It was dark and kind of creepy with all the lights off. The mannequins standing around in the back made it even worse, like they would come alive at any moment.

"Ugh." I shuddered. "So, weird."

"What is?" Ian looked over at me, his hands holding a pair of garters.

Rolling my eyes, I snatched the garters from his hands. "Stop touching stuff, you pervert. I mean the store. It's disturbing like this. Like someone's weird idea of a haunted house."

An arm slid around my waist and I was jerked against Ian's side. "Are you scared? You can hold onto me. I'll protect you." His magic slid down my arm and flicked my nipple.

Flushing, I pushed him away. "Knock it off. I thought we're here for revenge? I'm not screwing you in here, so you might as well get it out of your head."

Pouting, Ian dropped his arm. "Fine, ruin my fun." He strolled through the back room, his eyes searching around. "We'll need to cast a spell to see the unseen."

"Huh?"

"You do want to know who messed up your dress, right?" Ian peeked over his shoulder.

I nodded.

"Then do as I say." He clapped his hands together the sound echoing in the room, an unsettling silence falling over the area. "Close your eyes."

I started to do as he asked but then paused. "You're not going to do anything weird, are you?"

Ian rolled his eyes. "Ye of little faith."

Sighing, I did as he asked. "Now what?"

"Reach out with your magic now. Imagine it is like a blanket of power touching every inch of the room. Search for what you need. Something to tie the person to your dress." I reached for the ball of light inside of me then flattened and stretched it, pushing it out around me. "Now, open your eyes. What do you see?"

Blinking, I slowly peeked out from beneath my lashes. The room was coated in yellow light, almost so bright that it hurt my eyes. I skimmed around looking for something, anything that would link someone to the destruction of my dress. "I don't... wait a second... what's that?" I pointed a finger at a single glowing red strand of string, which was standing out from the rest of the yellow light. No, hair. I pushed past Ian and bent down to pick it up. "How will this help us?"

Ian plucked the hair from my hands and dropped it into a tube of liquid. Where the hell had that come from? I didn't get the chance to ask, my eyes focused on the liquid as he swirled it around the hair inside swimming around. Before my eyes, the contents of the tube changed colors from clear to dark blue.

"As I suspected." Ian closed his eyes and bopped his head.

"What?" I grabbed the tube from him. "What did you suspect?"

"That it was a witch."

"Well, duh." I shook my head. "We are in a witch shop. And besides, a guy would never bother to mess with my dress. They aren't that vindictive."

"You know a lot of guys?" Ian arched a brow, making me blush.

"Well, no, not really, just, you know. Guys are usually pretty upfront when they don't like someone. They're not likely to go around sabotaging someone like this." I waved a hand around the room. "But seriously, we went to all this trouble just to find out something I already knew?" I blew out a hard breath. "Lame."

Ian snatched the tube back from my hand. "Don't sell me short yet. I'm not done." He uncorked the top as I curiously watched on. Holding his hand out, he poured the contents into his hand, and then blew on it. The liquid transformed into a cloud of air, floating around in the air before us.

"What's that?" I gaped at the cloud.

"Just watch." Ian placed his hand on my head and forced my head to face the cloud. The inner part of the cloud warped, the gassy insides converting into an image of a person. "There." He lifted his hand off my head. "There's your answer."

I gaped at the cloud, not believing what I was seeing. "M...Monica?" She's the one who ruined my dress? But why?

Chapter 17

I COULDN'T FEEL MY tongue. I'd been sitting at the breakfast table for over ten minutes, and everything I'd put in my mouth had no flavor.

Eggs? Nothing. Toast? Nada. Even my coffee went down without my usual need for cream and sugar. I blamed it on the stress of it all. It had hindered my ability to process any information today.

Today. It was today. In a few short hours. My coming out party.

The day I would be announced to the magical community had come, far faster than I had expected. Okay, so that was a lie. It had been beaten into me every day since the day I agreed to have a coming out party.

With one disaster after another causing all kinds of havoc on my life, it wasn't hard to remember the whole point of it all.

All my problems had been fixed. The food was being taken care of by Aidan's parents, who I hadn't even had a chance to meet yet. I couldn't really picture what they would look like. The only adjective I could think of was... tall. One or both of them had to be huge to have a kid like Aidan.

I wondered if they were quiet too, or if he was quiet because they were loud? Also, did they have the same powers as him? Like was it hereditary or was it some rare ability that only one in a million magical babies acquired? It probably wasn't a good idea to ask about it right off the bat though.

Dealing with parents wasn't hard for me, not usually. Jaron's parents had been pleasant. I mean they weren't the Brady Bunch, but they weren't rude by any means. Callie's parents were divorced so they were always on their best behavior when I was over with Callie, each of them trying their hardest to buy their daughter's affection. Of course, Callie bathed in the attention and gifts. Sometimes those gifts passed onto me, and who was I to look a gift Gucci in the mouth?

I figured I'd meet the Templars when they came to set up for the party after lunch. I just hoped Aidan was there to make it a bit less awkward. Or, wait, would that make it even more awkward?

"You're thinking too hard," my grandmother's voice interrupted my thoughts. She stared at me over her teacup from her side of the table. "You're going to make yourself break out. It runs in the family. One ounce of stress and our skin revolts against us. It's rather unpleasant."

I gave her a weak smile. "Sorry, just worried about what else could go wrong." I held my tongue and didn't tell her that I suspected Monica behind it all. No need to bring it to light if I didn't know for sure.

"Well, don't. You have faced several problems already and came out more or less on top." My grandfather sat down his *Daily Scribe* on the table in front of him. The front page had an image of both of them with me sitting between them. The reporter had stopped by yesterday for the coming out announcement. If I'd known it was going to be on the front page, I might have smiled more.

Fortunately, my grandfather was right. Besides, the food, the music was being taken care of by Trina's older sister, Belinda. My dress had been saved by cousin Addy and was currently sitting up in my room with so many magic wards on it, the White House would be easier to break into.

Addy was staying at my parents but would come to help me with my hair and make up a bit later. She said something about not wanting to face the dragon before she had to. I deciphered dragon as my grandmother. Why did Addy think grandmother was a dragon?

"I need quite a bit more tequila to tell that story," Addy had told me when I'd asked.

Unfortunately, while my ducks were moving into a dutiful line, my biggest issue right now was my eyelids. I didn't get a wink of sleep last night. I kept thinking about Monica and why she would want to mess with my dress. I didn't have to guess how she knew about it. She had seen me in the dress with Sabrina. Did Sabrina make her do it?

God, I was tired. If my hand weren't holding my face up, I'd fall nose first into my plate. The last thing I needed was a bruised nose to go with my drooping lids.

"After breakfast, we should go to the ballroom and supervise the decorations," my grandmother continued as if everything had already been decided. "If you let those know-it-all goblins set everything up, you'll end up with the chandeliers on the dance floor and the ice sculpture on the ceiling."

"Goblins?" I arched a brow, thinking I was too sleep deprived to have heard her right.

"Oh, that's right." My grandmother put her teacup down, patting her lips with her napkin. "You haven't met any goblins yet have you?"

"Uh..." I tried to recall my recent encounter with goblins and could only remember the feel of Aidan's fingers thrusting deep inside of me. I hide my heated face behind my coffee cup, shaking my head. "Not really no."

"Well," my grandmother stood from her chair, "I will let you in on a little secret. The best way to deal with them is to not."

"Huh?"

"Come with me." She crooked a finger, and I climbed to my sock-covered feet. I hadn't even bothered to dress properly, just yoga pants and baggy t-shirts. Of course, grandmother had given me a once-over with a disapproving glower but kept her mouth shut as far as commenting. She was probably too happy that the party was finally here to pick at my outfit.

I allowed grandmother to lead me through the dining room and into the hallway. We went past the library and into the long hallway I'd already gotten lost in five times. There were so many doors that it wasn't hard. I couldn't imagine how it was going to be for the party tonight.

"Is everyone going to come this way?" I asked as we made our way into the ballroom.

My grandmother had been right. The room was already full of life. Goblins, the short creatures like the ones from Aidan's house raced around the room, each of them with different things in their arms. Flowers. Plates. Even a live swan. It squawked at us.

"Make sure you put that out in the yard." My grandmother waved a hand at the goblin and then turned back to me. "The hallway will be spelled, so the walk is shorter. We wouldn't want the guests to get lost, now would we?"

I chuckled along with her. Then she was on the move again. Socks sliding across the floor, I had to take small steps to keep myself from falling on my ass. Thankfully, my grandmother's attention was on the flower arrangements and not my ungraceful steps.

The ballroom was everything I had imagined it would be. Large columns led up to a vaulted ceiling. The dome above had been charmed so that during the day it showed a painted ceiling full of laughing and dancing cherubs actually moving around on the ceiling, and then turned transparent at night. Several large chandeliers floated unchained to the rafters, their gleaming jewels turning slowly in a circle.

"Don't stare too long at those, dear." My grandmother placed a hand on my arm. "Your mother once threw up from it. Not a pretty sight."

My nose wrinkled. "Ew."

"However, as I was saying..." My grandmother directed me over to a goblin. This one was much larger than the others, almost adult human height, except it was fatter and its head was kind of squashed into its shoulders. "This is Luke. He handles the goblin workers and makes sure they stay on task, else they run askew, and then we all end up with a fiasco like the Perriquinkles Bar Mitzvah." She and Luke shared a laugh. I laughed along with them though I had no idea what they were talking about.

"Luke this is my granddaughter, Maxine. She's the guest of honor. Please make sure your employees are aware of her and if she has any changes she'd like made."

Luke let out a gruff. "Yes, ma'am."

"Now, Max." My grandmother wrapped an arm around my shoulders and led me out of the ballroom. "I want you to go upstairs and take a nap. I'll send someone up to wake you when we need you. We don't want to start the night off with bags under our eyes, do we?"

She stopped us in the hallway to smooth her hands over my face. So much for thinking I was hiding exhaustion.

We started moving again back toward the front of the house. A nap sounded heavenly, but I wasn't sure I'd be able to sleep not with everything going on. "But what about getting ready? And Aidan's parents will be here any minute."

"Don't you worry, I'll take care of everything down here. You just get in a good hour or so and then into the shower with you." Grandmother gave me a little shove toward the stairs. "And please, make sure you are presentable when you come back down for lunch. You don't want to give the Templars the wrong impression now do we?" She gave me a tight smile that I forced myself to return before marching up the stairs.

I really didn't think I'd be able to sleep, even though I was dead tired. Maybe I could use some kind of spell to give me a pick me up or something?

"What are you doing?" I asked a maid who was pushing a cart into my room. It had a teapot and one cup on it.

The maid stopped in her tracks, turning with a smile. "Your grandmother requested I bring you something to help you sleep."

"Oh, thank you." I followed her into my room and took the cup she offered. It smelled of warm milk, lavender, and just hint of something spicy. Taking a sip, I hummed.

"Good?"

"Yes, it is. Thank you." I took the cup over to my bed, sitting beneath the covers. "Could you have someone wake me in an hour?"

The maid smiled. "That's what the tea is for. It is Timer Set Tea. It will put you to sleep and jolt you awake when the time is up."

"How does that work?" I asked, through a yawn. That tea meant business.

"By adding thyme of course." The maid smiled. "Just a pinch will do for a cat nap. Or a teaspoon for an hour. You don't want to use too much or..." I didn't hear the rest of her speech before my eyelids closed, and I was out like a light.

Just as abruptly, my eyelids shot open, and I sat up straight in my bed. It took me a second to figure out where I was and what I was doing. The teacup I'd been holding had been taken away as well as the cart. The maid had long since gone, probably the culprit behind the missing items.

I stretched and climbed out of bed. "Man, she wasn't kidding. I feel great." I checked the time on my phone. "Huh, one hour exactly."

Sometimes magic really was nifty.

With a bit of pep in my step, I made my way into the shower, and I destroyed some of the classics with my off-key singing while I washed. I didn't care though. I was in a good mood, and nothing was going to ruin it.

I kept my hair down and used a quick drying spell my mom had taught me before applying some light make up. Lip gloss. Mascara. Done. Feeling in a girlie mood, I pulled on a flower-covered sundress that tied around my neck. A pair of wedge sandals and I was ready for lunch.

Strolling down the stairs, I started for the dining room, but Charlie stopped me. "Lunch is being served on the terrace today."

"Thank you, Charlie." I smiled at the older man and then changed the direction of my feet. My hands were behind my back, and I had a bit of a sway to my step, I didn't think anything to darken my day.

Well, I was wrong.

"Oh, Max." Sabrina Craftsman beamed that large smile of hers at me. "There you are. We were beginning to think you might sleep the entire day away." She giggled with my grandmother, a glass of lemonade in her hand.

"Sabrina," I bit out, determined to keep my good mood, "I wasn't expecting you here so early."

"Please Max, have a seat," my grandmother urged me, not at all bothered by our exchange. "Sabrina has kindly offered to lend a helping hand. Seeing as she's helped plan several of these events before, we should welcome her assistance."

Sabrina and my grandmother smiled pleasantly at each other while my mom and Callie seemed ready to hara-kiri with their butter knives.

The chair at the table pulled out for me, and a plate floated from the buffet set up to the spot between the silverware. I took the seat offered, my hand going around my own butter knife.

"Well." I let out with a huff. "How nice. Don't you need to get ready for tonight? I know it takes a while for you to put on your face."

"Maxine," my grandmother admonished.

Sabrina only giggled. "Oh, Max. Such a joker." She tilted her head toward my grandmother. "She really does have such a profound sense of humor. Since she's dating four guys, she already knows what it means to be the butt of every joke. Or is that the whore?" She placed her hand over her mouth in mock embarrassment. "Did I say that out loud? My apologies. My mouth gets away from me when I'm nervous."

I scowled at her. Nerves, my ass.

However, my grandmother just lapped that shit up, not even jumping to my defense. My mom and Callie though. Man, if looks could kill.

"Oh!" Sabrina jumped up from the table, her lemonade suddenly knocking over and dumping into her lap.

I caught my mom's smirk and laugh hiding behind her napkin. At least, I always knew she had my back.

"Perhaps you should head on home now," I urged Sabrina with a megawatt smile. "You'll want to have plenty of time to get ready."

With a huff, Sabrina threw her hands up and walked into the house, thankfully leaving us to enjoy our lunch in peace.

"Now, that wasn't very nice," my grandmother admonished while I sipped from my glass. "You shouldn't make enemies with that girl. Her parents have heavy influence in the magical community."

I snorted. "She made a point to be enemies with me from day one. And besides that," I took a bite of the pasta salad on my plate, "dating her ex-boyfriend would have definitely put me in her non-friend box without ever talking to me.”

“Still, the girl may not be the most pleasant but blatantly insulting her is not wise.” Grandmother lifted her own fork to her mouth.

“And what she said about Max wasn’t insulting?” Mom argued, her eyes narrowed on my grandmother.

“Yeah, she called Max a whore,” Callie reminded and then mimicked Sabrina. “Oh, I’m sorry my mouth gets away from me when I’m nervous. What a fake. At least, Max is upfront about it.”

Callie and I shared a nod of solidarity.

My grandmother rubbed her temple. “Oh, goddess, give me strength. I thought I was done with these childish games when Margaret left.”

“Well, you wanted Max in your life.” My mom gave her a smug grin. “You got it.”

Grandmother didn’t have much else to say after that. My mom excused herself to go pick up my dad from the university. They’d be coming back later for the party, leaving me with Callie to get ready.

“The Templars are here. Didn’t you want to meet them?” my grandmother called up the stairs, stopping Callie and my ascent.

"Ooh," Callie clasped her hands together. "Does that mean that big one, what's his name, is here too?"

I rolled my eyes at her. "His name's Aidan. And probably." To my grandmother, I asked, "Are they in the kitchen?"

"Yes, and the Templars thankfully aren't known for having high standards so what you're wearing should be fine to meet them." She skimmed her eyes over my sundress, and I forced myself not to feel underdressed. My grandmother didn't wait for my response before leaving to do whatever it was she needed to do before the party.

"Jeez," Callie climbed down the stairs behind me. "I'd hate to know what you'd have to wear to meet someone with higher standards?"

I snorted. "Probably a full set of skirts and a corset." I stepped down the last couple of stairs and moved toward the kitchen. "Come on, let's go make nice with the parents. Hopefully, I don't stick my foot in my mouth and end up serving my guests live snails."

"Ew." Callie wrinkled her nose. "Sounds gooey." We fell apart in giggles as we pushed the kitchen door open.

The usual kitchen staff was nowhere to be seen and the rest of the kitchen had been taken over by...

"What are those?" Callie gaped at the small creatures with large noses and big ears.

"Goblins." I bumped her shoulder with a grin. "Don't worry, it freaked me out too."

Callie didn't answer, her eyes locked on the feisty creatures.

Patting her on the shoulder, I laughed. "I'm going to go find the chefs, try not to annoy any of them. I'm not exactly sure how well they respond to humans."

"Gotcha."

Not seeing Aidan anywhere, I searched for the only other people-looking people in the kitchen. A tall woman with blonde hair twisted up on top of her head stirred a pot on the stove. She released the spoon and picked up the salt and pepper, the spoon continuing to stir on its own. That must be Aidan's mom.

"Hi," I stepped up next to her. "I'm Max." The woman didn't answer, so I tried again. "My grandmother told me to come introduce myself, and seeing how I'm kind of dating Aidan, I thought that..." When the woman gave no indication of hearing me, I stopped talking. I glanced at her and then back to Callie who was trying to take selfies with the goblins and then back to the woman.

What the fuck?

When I was just about to try again, maybe wave a hand in her face, she turned around. A confused expression crossed her face and then a small smile curled up her lips. Her hand went up to her ear, where a small device sat in her ear. She flipped a twitched and said, "Sorry, I had my hearing aid off. It's easier to concentrate without all the…" She waved a hand at the scrabbling goblins. "…noise."

My mouth gaped open for a moment and then I clipped it shut. "Yeah, of course. I totally understand." I stared at her for a moment, not sure really what to say.

Thankfully, she saved me from further embarrassment. "You must be Max." She held her hand out for me to shake. "Aidan's told me so much about you."

I flushed and shook her hand. "All good, I hope."

"Oh, completely. I'm his step-mom, Diane." She twisted back toward the pot, turning a knob so the heat turned down. "Aidan's not here yet. He's helping his father bring in the other boxes. I'm so excited to go to a coming out party. It's my first."

"Mine too." I grinned and then cocked my head to the side. "You haven't been to a coming out party before?"

Diane smiled. "Oh, I've cooked for one but never actually been invited to one. Aidan's father and I have only been married for a few months now. I'm not exactly part of the group who gets invited to parties."

"Another thing we have in common." I turned and waved Callie over. "This is my best friend, Callie. She's human but knows about all this stuff." I gestured to Diane. "This is Aidan's stepmom, Diane."

They exchanged greetings, and we made small talk until Aidan and a large burly man came in through the back door. Of course. That's where Aidan got his linebacker build from.

"Aidan," Diane greeted, waving a hand over to us. "Look who I found or, well, found me." She embraced Aidan's dad, kissing him on the cheek. "This is my husband, Xander. This is Aidan's girlfriend, Max. Remember?"

Aidan's dad, Xander, was an intimidating man, even more so than his son when we first met. Except unlike Aidan, he didn't speak. At all. He didn't even offer me his hand or even a casual nod of acknowledgement.

Trying not to let it bother me, I turned to Aidan. Wringing my hands together, I peered up at him shyly. "Uh, I wanted to come say hi before my cousin Addy kidnaps me for pre-party fun."

Aidan's eyes sparkled with amusement. "You look pretty."

My eyes shot down to my dress and smoothed my hands over it. "Oh, yeah. Thanks. I woke up in a good mood and thought I'd just..." I flushed, tucking a strand of hair behind my ear.

"Hi, I'm Callie." She shoved her hand in Aidan's face. "The official best friend."

Shaking her hand, Aidan nodded. His blue eyes then moved back to me, he flicked his head to the side. I chewed on my lower lip and then bopped my head.

"I'll be right back," I told Callie and then smiled politely at Diane and Xander. "It was nice to meet you."

I took Aidan's hand and led him out of the kitchen and out onto the terrace. Leaning against the railing, I smacked my lips. "So, your dad seems nice."

Aidan grunted.

"I see where you get your talkative side from."

"He hasn't talked much since my mother died," Aidan told me, making me feel like a right ass.

"I'm sorry." I placed a hand on his shoulder, smoothing it up and down, my face leaning against it. "I didn't mean to pry."

"You didn't." He took my hand and brought it up to his lips. "It was a while ago. Diane has been good for him."

"And me?" I asked, moving closer to him so our chests brushed against each other. "Am I good for you?"

Aidan's lips twitched. "For my patience? No." His hand moved up to the back of my neck, cupping my head his lips close to mine. "But I'll live."

Chapter 18

"EVERY GIRL SHOULD HAVE her own tiara, I always say." Addy finished topping off my head with a small tiara filled with white jewels and offset by blue and purple ones.

I grinned up at her through the mirror. "It's great, Addy. I love it really. I couldn't have asked for anything better." I jumped to my feet and gave her a huge hug.

Addy laughed, wrapping her arms around me. "Oh, it's no trouble, dearie. I'm happy to help." She settled me back on my feet and adjusted her own hair in the mirror. "So, which one of your man candies is going to escort you in?"

My brow furrowed for a moment not sure what she means and then my eyes widened. Fuck. I knew I forgot something.

"Max?" Addy stared at me for a moment, concern etched on her face. "Honey, are you alright?"

Breathing heavily, my eyes darted from her to the mirror and back. I had the dress, the food, the music, even the god damn tiara but I had forgotten one crucial thing. Something everyone had been telling me to decide on, but I'd pushed it to the back of my mind not wanting to think about it.

Picking just one of them would have implications, implications I wasn't ready to face. Nor did I want to. I didn't want to pick one of the guys. I wanted all of them, now and for as long as they wanted to stay that way.

I had no grand illusions that something might come along and ruin the little arrangement we had, but I liked to think it would all end up alright in the end. Who said that it had to end now? Not me. Sure, as hell not me.

"I've got to go," I told Addy, dashing toward the bedroom door. In an afterthought, I paused at the door, looking back at the curious Addy. "I'm sorry, thanks again. I'll see you at the party."

"Don't worry about it, sweetie," she called after me, but I was already out the door and headed toward the stairs.

I passed by several goblins hustling to get the finishing touches on the house before the first guests arrived. I almost knocked one over in my hurry.

"Watch out!" the goblin snarled, waving a little fist at me.

"Sorry!" I waved a hand back at him in apology and then smacked right into one of the people I was searching for.

"Max, oh… fuck. You look good." Ian's lip curled into a wicked grin that, if I weren't in a hurry, would have melted my panties right off my body.

"Ha, thank you." I squirmed in his hands, my eyes scanning his own suited form. "Are the others here yet?"

"What, no kiss for me?" He arched a brow, and I wrinkled my nose at him before pushing onto my toes. I kissed him good and solid, careful not to smear my lipstick. "Well, that's no fun." He frowned. "I'd hoped to sneak in a quickie before the party."

Rolling my eyes at his teasing, I looped my arm through his. "Come on, show me where the others are. I need to talk to you all."

"About what?"

"You'll see soon enough." I grinned at him, feeling very much the Cinderella with him at my side.

"Ah, Max," my grandmother cooed at the bottom of the stairs. "Now, aren't you a sight? Why, I remember my coming out party! I was so excited. And your grandfather was dashing in his black suit and tie to match." Her eyes moved to Ian at my arm. "Is Mr. Broomstein going to escort you? If so, it's not too late to charm his tie to match."

I squeezed Ian's arm and then beamed down at my grandmother. "Actually, I was just about to talk to the guys about that. Have you seen them?"

She frowned slightly at my answer and then gestured to the parlor. "Your friend Trina has also arrived early. She said she had some news you've been waiting for?"

Curious about what Trina would have to say, I followed my grandmother into the parlor. When I stepped into the room, Paul, Dale, and Aidan all stood their eyes sweeping over me in appreciation. Trina sat next to Callie and my mom on the couch, while my dad stood by the window, tapping away on his phone.

"Hey," I greeted, not sure who to go to first.

Dale thankfully decided for me, coming over and pressing his lips to my cheek, whispering in my ear. "You look gorgeous."

"Thank you." I flushed, releasing Ian's arm to embrace him for a moment.

Aidan had already been here with his parents for a few hours, so I went to Paul instead. "You look great." I gestured at his suit. "If I didn't know any better, I'd say you guys have done this before." A collective laugh followed my comment.

Paul kissed me on the side of the mouth, being careful not to smudge my makeup before taking a step back. He seemed uncomfortable with PDA in front of my parents but kept his hand on my waist nevertheless.

I looked to Trina, who was looking great in her form-fitting black dress. "Grandmother said you had something to tell me?"

"Ah, yeah." She stood and pulled her phone out. "You remember how all the caterers were booked? And then the music and your dress?"

"Yeah?" I arched a brow at her wondering where she was going with all this.

"And remember how your booth at the Spring Fair got destroyed? And no one saw anything?" I nodded. She was really starting to freak me out. Especially, when she made such a fearsome face. "Well, apparently those weren't coincidences."

Moving away from Paul to where she held her phone up, I frowned. "What am I looking at here?"

Trina shook her phone and let out an impatient huff. "All the caterers were booked by the same person for a fake event by the Magenski family."

"The who?" I arched a brow, looking around at the others for some clue as to what she was talking about.

Paul bumped my arm. "Magenski. As in Monica Magenski?"

A light clicked on in my head. "What? You think Monica has something to do with this?"

"Yep." Trina popped her p's. "And that's not all." She gestured to my mom, who handed her phone over. "She was also behind the destruction of your dress." She played a video on my mom's phone. It seemed to be some kind of security footage. I recognized the interior of Madame Lace's dress shop, and there was Monica sneaking around like she was afraid to be caught wielding a pair of scissors and an eager sneer on her face. I watched her rip into my dress with such a fierceness that I had to look away. It was just too cruel.

"So, Monica's out to get you?" Dale mused. "I mean, it makes sense."

"What we saw at the store makes sense now," Ian mused, rubbing his jaw.

"What you saw? When did you go back to the store?" my mom asked, suspicion in her eyes.

"Yesterday," I told her. "We found a hair and did a spell. It showed Monica as the probable culprit, but what I don't understand is why?" I turned my head toward Dale. "She's been nothing but nice to me. I'd have believed Sabrina or even Libby, no offense, Trina, before I'd ever have suspected Monica."

"That's exactly why it's so diabolical," Callie announced jumping to her feet. "It's smart if you think about it. You never see the dagger coming."

"What?" I gave her a dubious look. "I think someone's been watching too many movies."

"Well, it's not that far off," Dale interjected, his arms crossed over his chest. He was looking dapper in his suit, his hair brushed back. All the guys were looking good tonight, and here I thought I'd be the one having a challenging time keeping their hands off me. I felt like a cat in heat wanting to rip their clothes off.

"What do you mean?" I asked, discreetly wiping the drool off my chin.

Dale cleared his throat, adjusting his stance. "When you think about it, the Magenskis have always been anti-human. It would only make sense that she would be guning for you." I frowned at his presumptions. "You are human-raised, getting special attention from not just the community but her best friend. Then came your booth at the Spring Fair."

My grandmother who had been listening quietly at the edge of the room took this moment to speak up. "The Magenskis are esteemed members of our society. I hardly think they care about a college student's coming out party or even her school project."

"Dale is right." Aidan broke his silence, turning our attention to him. He had that far off look in his eyes that signaled he'd just had a vision.

"What do you see?" Ian tucked his hands into his pants pockets, a scowl on his face.

"The Magenski girl used a perception charm at the fair." He crossed his large arms over his chest, the muscles tensing beneath the skin.

"Okay, so Monica is a class-A bitch. Got it." I threw a thumbs up toward them, my mind still reeling with the new information. I had to admit I felt a bit betrayed. I mean, Monica and I weren't the closest of friends. We barely knew each other. However, I still hated liars and phonies. Sabrina might put on a front for her parents, but at least she was upfront with her hatred for me. But Monica pretending to be my friend just so she could screw with me? That was so not cool.

Aris bopped by my head. That's right. Way not cool.

"Max?" Callie touched my arm. "Are you sure you're okay?"

I shrugged her off, offering her my biggest smile. "I am. Don't worry about it. I don't want it to ruin our night." Turning to the rest of the room, I gestured toward my dad to get off his phone. "And while I have you all here, I have an announcement I'd like to make."

When I had everyone's attention, I shifted so that I was next to the guys. I pulled Dale and Paul over to stand with Ian and Aidan. "I know everyone has been asking me who I'm going to have to escort me tonight. I haven't been shy about what my thoughts are on the subject." My grandmother made a rude sound, but I ignored her. "I know choosing someone to present me to the magical community is a big deal. It not only aligns me with that person's family but also tells everyone that I have the intentions..." I softly smiled at the guys. "... of one day marrying them."

The mix of expression before me didn't do anything to dissuade me from my big moment. "So, I thought long and hard on who should escort me, and I've decided..." The tension in the room was palpable and I swear my grandmother was holding her breath. "... that I'm not choosing any of them."

"What?" my grandmother's voice rose, echoing in the room. "You can't just do that. It's not heard of. Do you know what people will say if you show up alone? At least have your father escort you!" She gestured an arm at my dad who didn't seem too thrilled by the prospect. He'd never been the kind to want to be the center of attention.

I rolled my eyes. "If you would let me finish, I wasn't done."

"Oh," my grandmother's eyes widened, and then with a sardonic smile, she waved an arm in front of me. "By all means, your highness. Please continue."

Ignoring her sarcasm, I stuck my tongue between my teeth and faced the guys. "What I was going to say was that I'm not just choosing one of you. I want all of you to walk me out tonight. Because I care about you, all of you, and I want everyone to know it."

It was Aidan's face that I noticed first. The usual stoic expression he kept on his face had broken. And not just one of his little half smiles but a full-on dimples-flashing, toothy grin. He even out beat Ian with his panty melting grin. It was so good.

"Hey, stop that." Ian elbowed Aidan. "None of us can get a look in with you flashing that crap around." Aidan chuckled and dimmed his lips drooped slightly.

Paul didn't say anything. He walked over to me and wrapped his arms around me. Either not caring my dad was watching, or despite it, he kissed me full on the mouth, not letting me go until Dale cleared his throat.

Releasing me to Dale, Paul blew me a kiss and took his place back by his brother. Dale took my hand in his and half bowed kissing my fingertips. I sort of giggled in return at his actions.

"I'd be honored to escort you."

"We all would be," Ian added on to Dale's words.

"This is going to be great." Callie clapped her hands giddily, her brown hair bouncing in the curls she'd put in it. Trina laughed at her side, a bit too pleased with herself.

"Well, I think it is ridiculous." My grandmother sniffed, crossing her arms defiantly. "After all the work, money, and time I put into making this a special day for you and you're going to ruin it all with this..." She waved a hand at us. "... sideshow."

"Mother," my mom came between us with a proud grin on her lips, "I think I speak for everyone when I say, get over it. You couldn't control me, and you're not going to control my daughter. I don't know why you ever thought you could."

My grandmother blew a harsh breath out through her teeth. "I don't know why I even bother. You're going to do what you want no matter what." She waved a wild hand at the guys and me. "What are you going to do when one of these young men gets her pregnant? How will you know who the father is? Will one of you marry her?"

Dale and Paul held my hands while Ian and Aidan stood at my back. "Well, I think that's an us problem. Not a you problem. Now, if you want me to be in your life, you have to accept that I'm not going to play by your rules."

"Then whose rules are you playing by?" my grandmother sniffed.

I laughed. "Hell, if I know. I'm making this up as I go along. And so far," I smiled softly at the guys. "I think I'm doing pretty damn good."

Chapter 19

A LARGE SET OF double doors was all that stood between the party and us. The music from the inside poured out through the walls, making my blood dance in my veins.

Trina's sister Belinda knew how to play. I had no doubt the music was making my grandmother and her older friends grimace. They were no doubt muttering under their breaths about kids and their loud music, but I didn't care.

This was my day, and I wasn't letting anyone ruin it.

"Are you ready?" My mom pressed in at my elbow. "Your dad and I are heading in."

I bobbed my head. "Yep." I glanced around at my four handsome guys. "I think I'm good."

Laughing, she gave me a sideways hug. "I have no doubt about that." To the guys around me, she pointed a finger. "You take care of her. There might be more of you, but I've been doing magic a lot longer."

I grinned at her defensive tone. "Thanks, mom."

Dad snuck between the guys and embraced me. "You look beautiful, and I'm so proud of you for standing up for yourself." His eyes slowly moved to the men around me. "And I don't have to make threats because you and I both know how devious your mom can get."

We shared a chuckle as my men watched on. They didn't seem the least bit worried, but it was good to know my parents had my back.

Taking a deep breath, I adjusted my skirt and checked my tiara to be sure it was still pinned to my hair. My fingers wiggled at my side and sort of bounced in place. My parents went through a side door, leaving me at the front for my big entrance. I'd been giddy about it all until now. Now though, my nerves decided to show.

A warm hand slid into my sweaty palm and squeezed it. I tilted my head up to meet Aidan's firm gaze and said, "I'm alright."

"How do you want to do this?" Ian asked, sliding an arm around my waist. "We could lift you up above our heads?"

Paul scoffed. "Leave it to you to pick the weirdest of options."

"What do you suggest we do?" he shot back at his brother.

"We could simply walk at her sides," Dale suggested. "Two in front, two in back, her in the middle, or would that be showing favoritism?"

"No, I like that." I gave him a shy smile, not wanting the others to argue. "But who gets to be where?"

"Pick a number," Aidan offered up.

"Okay." I cocked my head to the side. "The two closest stands in front, the other two in back."

Ian snickered. "Sounds like my kind of party."

Rolling my eyes at him, I thought of a number. Seventeen. That's a pretty good number.

"Pick between one and twenty." I turned to Dale first.

"Eight."

Then Ian. "Nineteen."

Paul next. "Twelve."

And lastly, Aidan. "Seventeen."

I narrowed my eyes at him. "You didn't use your powers, did you?"

"Of course not." His lips ticked up at the edges, making me not believe him completely.

"Fine." I decided to leave it alone. No time to argue. "Ian and Aidan in front. Paul and Dale in back."

"Sounds good to me." Dale smirked, and Ian jumped up to my side. "Shall we?"

I took a deep breath. "Yeah, I think so."

With a flick of their wrists, the door opened. The music faltered for a moment and then the song we had decided on for my entry began. It was light and bubbly. Just how I wanted it.

The crowd parted as we stepped into the room. The first set of eyes on me were my parents. They gave us an encouraging thumbs up. My grandparents, well, my grandfather lifted his glass to me while my grandmother managed to keep a straight face. That woman could beat anyone at poker, I swear.

There was a collective gasp and then a tittering through the crowd as they realized I had not one escort but four. Lifting my chin a bit higher, I made my way into the middle of the room. I caught sight of cousin Addy near both of my best friends. She inclined her head at me with a big grin, thoroughly enjoying the drama my men and I were causing.

Stopping in the middle of the ballroom, I nodded to those watching. Ian turned first, taking my hand in his and pressing his lips to my fingers. Then Aidan, with his large hands and massive shoulders. More than a few women were already eying him. Dale followed Aidan as I spun around to face them. Paul was last. He bowed before taking my hand. His mouth brushed across the knuckles of my hand and then he straightened.

Standing at his side stood my dad. Paul handed me over to him, and the music changed. The waltz began, and we took our places. Moving around the room, I tried to focus on my dad's face and not the people staring.

"I think that went rather well." My dad grinned at me. "Don't you?"

I let out a harsh breath. "Well, no one is throwing fruit or running from the room screaming."

My dad's hand squeezed my waist. "The night is young."

Giggling, I let myself enjoy my first dance with my dad. Normally, that dance would be with the man who escorted me, but since I had four escorts... well... it was just easier for my dad to do it. I wasn't a great dancer. I'd save my boyfriends' feet for one night.

Eventually, the rest of the room stopped staring, and others joined us on the dance floor. My dad led me off the floor when the song ended and handed me over to my group of guys. Dale held out a glass of some pink liquid which I took but didn't drink.

"What's in this one?" I asked warily.

With a knowing laugh, Dale shook his head. "It's just champagne. I promise, no magic."

My lips still twisted in a distrusting frown, I took a hesitant sip. When the familiar carbonated alcohol touched my throat, I took an even bigger drink. When Professor Morison walked up to me, I almost choked on my drink.

"Max," he greeted in his real accent, taking a look at the group around me. "I half expected you to let your grandmother turn this into another one of those boring events where everyone is talking about how much money they have or the latest issue of Witch's Weekly." He chuckled, taking a drink of his glass. "But everyone can't stop talking about you and your men."

"Well, what can I say?" I clucked my tongue. "I'm just chock full of gossip for the masses." I started to ask him something, but

Callie bumped my arm, almost dumping my drink. Scowling over my shoulder at her, I sighed. "Professor Morison have you met my best friend, Callie?"

"Hi," she pushed forward between us. "So, you're from England?"

Morison chuckled. "Yes, but now I teach Etiquette of Magic at the school. Are you a student there?"

"No way," Callie beamed. "I go to Brown. I'm human." That was Callie for you. Not at all ashamed of who she was not even if she was one of the sole humans in a room full of witches and wizards.

"Well, then." Morison offered her his arm. "You can call me Rupert."

"Alright, Rupert." She took his arm and then winked at me, mouthing 'oh my god.'

I giggled as I watched them walk away, Callie chatting his ear off. I just knew it was a matter of time before she found a wizard to latch onto, I just never figured it would be one of my professors. Turning around to watch the room, I hummed. "So, how long do you think?"

"How long until what?" Paul asked, turning from Callie who he had been speaking with to me.

"Until someone freaks out on us," I replied with a cheeky grin. "I'm surprised one of your parents hasn't come by and accused me of bespelling you all."

Aidan blew a puff of air out through his nostrils. It sounded a bit like a horse huffing.

"You don't think they will?" I glanced over my shoulder at him.

"I think our parents are the least of your worries."

I didn't have a chance to ask him about what he meant before an annoyingly chipper voice called my name. Monica Magenski appeared before me with a man I didn't recognize at her arm. She wore a white dress quite similar to the one she'd destroyed. A quiet way of telling me she was the culprit?

"I'm having so much fun at your party." Monica giggled, shifting from side to side as if she couldn't stay in one spot. "And the look on everyone's face when you entered?" She let out a hyena laugh and looked to her date. "It. Was. Priceless."

I arched a brow at her and then to my guys who looked about ready to rip her bouncing head off. I shook my head at them, silently telling them that I would handle it.

"Monica, I think you should leave." I tried to do it the polite way, but she didn't seem to take the hint.

"Why?" Monica's brows shot up to her hair line. "We just got here, why would I want to leave?"

"You're not welcome here." Paul crossed his arms over his chest, his eyes narrowing on her. "You should take the chance to leave now before you make a scene."

"A scene?" Monica scoffed. "Why would I make a scene?"

"Wow, she is one good liar." Dale adjusted the cuffs of his suit. "I guess it runs in the family."

Monica's brown eyes darted from each of my guys and then back to me, worry etching her face. "I really don't know what you're talking about, and in any case, I can't leave. My parents are here, and if I left, they'd want to know why, and I can't deal with that kind of drama right now."

"Fine," I snapped. "If you don't want to leave on your own, I guess I'll just have to tell everyone what a nasty little human hater you are."

"What?" Her voice went up to an annoyingly high pitch. "I don't hate humans. Why would I?" I stared at her for a long moment, trying to figure out what kind of game she was playing. "I don't like that look on your face. Why are you looking at me like that?"

"Kind of like the look on your face when you were destroying my dress?" I asked, enjoying the way her smile wilted. "Now, that was something to see."

"What are you talking about? I didn't touch your dress." She brushed her hair behind her ear, her eyes not able to focus on me. "You know, I had wondered why you picked this one instead of the white one, though this one is even better."

Magic billowed up inside of me drawn by my anger and hurt, making my words burn as they came out. "You know, I thought you were my friend, Monica. I thought, hey, there must be some redeeming qualities about Sabrina if Monica was friends with her. But it looks like it was you that I should have been worried about."

Monica's head moved from side to side, disbelief on her face. "I... I don't know what you are talking about." Her voice had gone to a high-pitched squeal.

"I think you know very well." I stalked toward her, making her stumble backward, drawing the attention of others around us. My grandmother was going to kill me for causing a scene at my own party nonetheless. "I know it was you who tried to ruin my coming out party, and I know it was you who sabotaged my booth at school.”

“No, no. That wasn’t me.” She still tried to deny it. “You’re wrong. A liar. She’s a liar.” She pointed a finger at me, trying to get the crowd on her side. “I don’t hate humans, and I have no reason to want your party ruined. We’re friends.”

“No, we’re really not.” I contemplated all the different things I could do to her. I could send her away, but that would require a transportation spell, something I hadn’t mastered yet. I wanted her gone not split in two, which was likely to happen if I tried something like that without training.

“What’s going on here?” Sabrina pushed through the crowd, coming to stand by her friend’s side.

I didn’t turn my gaze from the crying traitor as I answered Sabrina. “You should pick your friends more wisely. This one is likely to stab you in the back when you’re not looking.”

Sabrina glanced between Monica and me. When her eyes landed on the brunette, Monica tried to latch onto her.

“Sabrina, you have to believe me. I’d never do anything to hurt you or anyone. She’s the filthy liar. She took your Paul and the rest of them, leaving nothing for anyone else.”

Once she started talking, it seemed she couldn't stop. "Why does she deserve all this? Why should we bow down to her? She might be a Mancaster, but she's no better than those disgusting humans she hangs around with." She pointed a finger at Callie. "See? She's already breaking all the rules. We would never have let someone like that in one of our events, but here we have not one but two humans and who knows how many others."

"Monica." Sabrina's voice caused the simpering girl to be quiet. "Shut up." Sabrina then turned away and walked back through the crowd, completely turning her back on Monica and her ranting.

Her mouth gaped open as she watched Sabrina walk away and then her eyes narrowed on me. Aris bounced around my head, letting off a ringing sound that was really rather late because I could see Monica's eyes narrow and feel the air around us thicken with power.

She shoved power at me. At that moment, a goblin with a tray of blueberry whipped tarts walked between us, completely oblivious to what was going on. The power hit the goblin and threw him across the room. His tray's contents flew through the air and covered several guests in their blue filling.

It seemed like going the nice way wasn't going to work with this one. I sighed. Why can't anything in my life just be simple for once?

Not wanting to hurt the crying woman but not sure how else to handle her, I had an idea. I drew the magic that had come up and pushed it out toward the screaming witch. Imagining the bubble as Dale had taught me, I focused on wrapping it around her rather than the room.

Her screaming was cut off as the bubble finished closing around her. Modifying the magic to solidify the bubble, I grinned as Monica tried to get out of it but ended up bouncing off the sides.

"Nice trick," Ian commented.

I winked. "I'm not done yet."

I urged the magic to become weightless and it lifted off the floor, taking Monica with it. Her silently screaming face was a sight to see and caused the crowd to murmur amongst themselves once more. She tried to throw a spell but whatever magic she was going to hit me with bounced back at her, making her face scrunch up in pain. Well, that solved whether or not she was the violent type. Though, the way she wailed on my dress with scissors had already hinted at that.

"Would you look at that?" Dale mused beside me. "You really do listen."

I stuck my tongue between my teeth and winked. "Despite some people distracting me." I glanced around the room and noticed we still had a crowd. "Alright, everyone. Back to the party nothing to see here." They didn't listen.

My grandmother barreled through the crowd, apologizing as she moved. "You," she pointed at a goblin, "get this mess cleaned up. Patricia?" She found my mom standing off to the side. "Do you think you can handle a simple cleaning spell?"

"Of course, mother." My mom narrowed her eyes at her before helping to clean up the guests who had been sprayed.

"You heard my granddaughter, get back to the party or you're going to be joining Miss Magenski on the ceiling." Turning away from the crowd, my grandmother's eyes settled heavily on me. "I should have known better than to hope for an uneventful evening from you."

I grinned cheekily. "Well, you know me."

"Yes," she said drily. "Unfortunately, I do. Try to behave yourself the rest of the night?"

She raised a brow at me and then walked toward the guests near my mom.

I stopped a goblin passing by with a tray of crackers and something colorful fizzing on top, I said, "Can you guys see if you can get Miss Magenski off the ceiling and back to her car?"

The goblin grunted before shuffling away.

"I'm going to take that as a yes." Turning back to the guys, I frowned. "Where'd Ian and Paul go?"

Aidan and Dale shrugged.

Seeing as they weren't bothered and Aris didn't freak out, I shrugged as well. "Alright, let's get some food in my stomach. All these things they're serving are weird. Did your parents make anything normal? Like pigs in a blanket?" I moved through the room and toward the kitchen entrance.

Dale grabbed my arm, stopping me. "There's something I think you'll like over here." He drew me over to the buffet table where there was a full spread of human and magical food.

I had my mouth crammed with my third piece of some chicken that was literally on fire when Aidan came up to me a concerned expression on his face.

"What is it?" I swallowed hard, coughing as a piece of food got stuck in my throat. "Did

Monica get back in?” I glanced up at the ceiling which had been void of Monica’s bubble for a good half hour.

“No.” Aidan took my plate and sat it on the table. “It’s Ian.”

Frowning, I let Aidan lead me away from the table and toward the terrace. “What’s wrong with Ian?”

“I had a vision.”

“What kind of vision?” I scanned around the yard but only saw darkness. “Dark magic kind of vision?”

Aidan nodded.

Rubbed my hands on my skirt, I gestured to Aidan. “Well, let’s go. I didn’t get all dolled up to have Ian’s new friends ruin it.” Aidan took my hand, and we fled the party and into the darkened yard below.

Chapter 20

MY HEART POUNDED IN my chest as we raced from the party and into the backyard. I hated thinking that Ian had gotten hurt in some way, especially after we talked to him about how dangerous his new friends could be.

"Where is he?" I asked Aidan, not able to see in the dark yard. "I thought you said he was out here?"

"He is," Aidan responded. Okay, so two words answers were his norm, but even I found that cryptic.

"Well, then?" I turned back to him gesturing helplessly. "Want to help a girl out? ESP it or whatever?"

Aidan chuckled. "It doesn't—"

"Work that way, yeah, yeah. I remember." I waved him off, my eyes squinting in the dark. "So, what exactly is he doing?

Summoning a demon? Bringing Alan Rickman back to life?"

"Not exactly."

I took several purposeful steps toward the edge of the pond in my grandparents' backyard. It wasn't lake-sized, I couldn't ride a ski boat across it, but it did have an adorable gazebo living in the middle of it. Not that I'd be able to get to it. There weren't any bridges or stepping stones.

However, someone was standing in the middle of it.

"There's someone over there," I muttered, moving closer to the edge.

"Is there?" Aidan came up behind me, so close I could feel his body heat. "Ian?"

I shook my head. "I don't know. I can't tell." The edge of my shoe touched the water, and I ignored the coolness coming through. "Maybe if we could get a bit closer?"

"Hold on." Aidan's large hand wrapped around my waist, pulling me back. "You're going to get wet."

I leaned my head back to look at him. "Do you really think now is the time to worry about my dress? It'll dry. However, a zombie apocalypse waits for no dress. In fact..." I tried to reach behind me to undo the dress.

"What are you doing?"

At Dale's voice, I startled falling sideways in my struggle against my dress. I almost face planted into the water, but Aidan thankfully caught me in time with his big hands.

"Trying to take my dress off so I can see if that's Ian over there and stop the warrior demons from taking over the human race and making us into their taco slaves."

"Wait, what?" Dale's brows furrowed. "I know something in there made sense, but I'm having difficulties deciphering it. Once more, for the little people?"

I snorted. Little people. Yeah right.

"Ian has gotten into some bad juju, and we're here to save the day," I summarized, still trying to get my dress undone. Giving up with a frustrated growl, I spun around. "Help me with the zipper."

"Hold on. That's not necessary." I glanced over my shoulder to see Dale scowl at Aidan. "Were you really going to let her strip down for this?"

Aidan smirked.

Shaking his head, Dale moved past me to the edge of the pond. Cupping his hands around his mouth, he shouted, "It's time."

"Time?" I glanced between the two of them. "Time for what?"

Dale pushed his glasses up his nose and smiled. "Just watch."

Aidan wasn't much help either. He moved to the other side of me and crossed his arms over his chest, waiting for something.

Glancing up at Aris, I scowled. Something funny was going on here. If Aris wasn't freaking out, then the real danger was not here. Or anywhere near here. Which only meant that...

The dark figures in the gazebo moved and the pond lit up. Water filled columns of light shot up from the pond in two straight lines, creating a sort of bridge toward the gazebo. The dark gazebo no longer covered by darkness, and as that veil pulled away, it revealed two people. Ian and Paul. They stood next to a table with a large cake and several packages.

It dawned on me that I'd been duped. "Ian wasn't in trouble, was he?" I glowered at Aidan halfheartedly.

He shrugged. "Only to himself."

"And you." I pointed a finger at a smiling Dale. "You had a hand in this?"

"We all did." Dale wrapped an arm around my shoulders. "With some help from your grandparents, of course."

"Of course." I murmured, though the fact that my grandmother had helped astounded me more than anything. She had been pretty clear about her feelings regarding all of my guys that the thought of her helping them do anything was a bit bizarre.

"So, how do we get over there?" I asked, staring down at the water. "I don't suppose you have a boat?"

"Actually," Dale waved his arm forward. The ground vibrated beneath our feet and panels of wood from beneath the pond rose up and formed a bridge, the water columns careening over it to form a series of arches.

I stared in awe as I made my way onto the bridge. When I stood underneath the columns of water, my shoulders bunched expecting to get wet. However, the water didn't even drip onto the bridge. It stayed above us in their own little tubes of light.

"This is really amazing," I murmured and then smiled back at Aidan and Dale who trailed behind me. "You did this all for me?"

Dale rubbed the back of his neck. "Well, you almost ruined it with that whole thing with Monica but yeah. It's your birthday after all."

My lips tipped down. "How did Monica almost ruin it?"

This time it was Paul who answered. "Not so much what she did, but after you dealt with her and then you ran into the kitchen, you almost caught us bringing the cake out here. Then the whole thing would have been for nothing." He offered me his hand.

I flushed, taking the hand he held out to me. "Well, it's not my fault. Kicking ass makes me hungry." I huffed and then sat down at the table next to Ian. "I see you're alive and well." I narrowed my eyes into slits looking for any signs that he had been doing something bad. "Was this your idea?"

Ian quirked a brow. "Well, I can't say it wasn't partly my idea, at least to use me as bait."

"The cake was Aidan's idea." Paul took the seat next to me, sandwiching me between the two brothers. "The whole light show was Dale."

"And what did you bring to this whole fiasco?" I peered up at Paul.

Paul grinned cheekily. "That." He pointed a finger behind me just as a loud boom filled the sky.

Spinning in my chair, I gaped at the fireworks being shot from the other side of the pond. I had seen dozens of human fireworks. They got boring once you hit puberty, but nothing prepared me for magical fireworks.

The rocket shot to the sky and burst into a large star. Instead of dispersing and falling to the ground, the sparks of fire rearranged their shape into a message.

Happy Birthday, Max.

"Ah, you guys," I cooed, tearing up against my better judgment. "This is so sweet."

"We just wanted to let you know that we're in." Paul kissed my forehead, making me frown.

"You're in?"

Dale stepped forward. "What you said before with your parents about caring about us all. We just wanted to make it official. We're all in. Whatever you want to do, we're here."

Aidan grunted his agreement.

Ian grabbed my hand, pulling me into his embrace. "If you want to keep dating all of us, that's fine. We're good with it. We do have some conditions though."

I raised a brow at him. "Conditions? I thought it was whatever I wanted to do?"

Aidan snorted, and I shot him a glare.

"What we meant was," Ian placed his hand on my face turning my eyes back to his, "that we're ready to share you equally, but you have to give equally as well." His finger stroked the side of my face.

I squinted at him. "Is this about sex? Because I thought we were doing pretty good on that front."

"We are." Ian nodded firmly. "However, it isn't just about sex. It's about—"

"Time," Aidan interjected. "Emotion."

"Dates," Paul added.

I glanced at Dale who hadn't said anything. "What, nothing from you?"

Dale smirked and then shot me a wink. "I'm just here for the sex."

I wrinkled my nose at him. "Oh, are you?"

The guys laughed together and then I put my hand up, stopping them. "I have conditions as well."

"Oh, you do?" Ian growled. "And having four of the most powerful wizards on campus at your beck and call isn't enough?"

"Pfft." I rolled my eyes. "I'll believe it when I see it."

Paul gestured to the cake and set up.

"Okay, fine. You're getting up there with the best boyfriends award, but I still have conditions." I put a finger up. "No fighting for my time. We can make a schedule or whatever if you want, but I'm not scheduling sex." I pointed a finger at Dale. "That's one thing I'd rather be organic, spontaneous."

"Very well." Aidan nodded.

"What else?" Paul placed his hand on my leg and wiggled it.

"Also, while I might be dating four of you, I don't want you with anyone else." I held my breath on that one. I knew it was selfish. I was asking them to be monogamous, but I wasn't. They'd totally tell me to fuck off.

"Fine by me," Ian announced with a grin, "as long as Paul makes out with me." He gave his brother a lewd wink which made Paul jump to his feet.

"No, no way. I'll keep to one-on-one sessions from now on, thank you." He held his hands up a look of pure disgust on his face.

Shaking my head as I laughed, I pushed at Ian. "Don't be mean. You don't want to kiss him any more than he wants to kiss you. I had a hard enough time getting you in the same bed naked."

Ian opened his mouth to make a comment, but Paul pointed a finger at him. "Don't even."

"What?" He raised a defensive shoulder. "I wasn't going to say anything."

"Yes, you were," Paul accused. "New rule. Anything that has to do with my dick or the size thereof should never come from my brother's mouth."

Dale and Aidan looked at the brothers with amusement. Ian, of course, couldn't let it go.

"What can I say? My brother is toting a toddler in his pants. I'm just supposed to ignore that?"

Paul's face colored redder than the frosting on the cake in front of us. Putting his hands over his ears, Paul shook his head. "I'm not listening. Tell me when he's done or I'm jumping ship. I don't care how deep this pond is."

We all laughed, and Ian finally stopped torturing his little brother. Cutting into the cake, we stuffed our faces while watching the rest of the fireworks.

"So," Dale asked after we'd finished eating, "did you have a third?"

"A third what?" I asked, sticking my finger in the frosting and then licking it off. Four pairs of eyes watched the movement and a ball of smug satisfaction filled my chest.

"A third rule?" Dale's eyes stayed transfixed on my finger as I slid it in and out of my mouth.

"Oh." I pulled my finger out with a loud pop. "Hmm, I didn't really have a number three, but I could think of one."

"Fuck no." Paul shook his head. "I'm good with those two rules."

"Me too." Dale raised a hand.

"I'm not." Ian leaned back in his chair and watched us. "I want to see what else is in that dirty little mind of hers."

A slow grin slid over my lips. "Okay, I have something." The others tensed as I watched Ian. "Though, it's more of a request than a rule. Think of it as a birthday present."

"Oh, a request? I like the sound of that." Ian arched a brow while Paul groaned.

Before I could open my mouth and tell them, Aidan swooped in and planted one right on Ian's mouth, tongue and everything. I gaped at them for a moment as I watched the two of them make out. I didn't snap out of it until Aidan pulled away.

"Hey, no fair," I whined. "You ruined the fun of asking for it."

Aidan lifted a shoulder. "I saw it two minutes ago."

"So," I pouted, ducking my head, "the whole point is to see the shock on everyone's face."

"Do you want to ask now?" Ian wiped the back of his hand over his mouth. "Because I could go again."

"Please don't." Paul made a gagging sound. "Seeing my brother make out with his best friend is a bit too much for me."

"Well, he could always make out with you." Ian grinned, and Aidan moved faster than anyone expected with his size.

Paul saw him coming for him and shook his head with pure terror on his face. "No way. Keep your lips to yourself."

Aidan and Paul darted around the gazebo for a second before Paul stepped off. Instead of falling in the water, he hovered just over the surface.

"I'm not coming back up there until that one swears to keep his lips to himself." Paul pointed a rigid finger at Aidan.

Laughing until my stomach hurt, I waved Aidan off. "Stop it already. Leave the poor guy alone. Besides, there's plenty of time for him to warm up to you." I arched a brow at Paul who cursed.

"I have a feeling we're going to be doing a lot of things we wouldn't normally do because of you," Dale mused though he didn't seem at all bothered by it.

The rest of them seemed to agree which was a-okay with me. I could use a few more compromises in my life. I'd done enough of my own recently. Time for life to give back to me.

Chapter 21

I WOULD LIKE TO say the rest of my summer was just as eventful as the first.

It wasn't.

It was really boring actually.

Before I knew it, school had started back up, and I was back in my dorm room, unpacking things.

"Hey, Max," Trina greeted, pushing our dorm room door open.

I shot a scowl at Aris. We really needed to work on those warnings. Sure, Trina wasn't a threat but was it too much to ask for a little bob? A little weave?

"Surprised to see you here already." Trina drew my attention back from my defective guardian light.

"Really?" I grinned. "Tomorrow is the first day of our second year, I wouldn't want to miss that."

"But now that you're Miss Popularity not just at school but in the magical community, I would think you'd be jetting around to rub brooms with your loyal fans." Trina winked at me and then hefted her suitcase back onto her bed.

"Jeez, what do you have in there?" I chuckled as she unbuckled the suitcase and pushed it open.

"Just books, shoes, and some clothes Belinda grew out of." She shrugged a shoulder as a massive number of things came falling out of her bag. One of those things looked like a paint ball gun.

"Why do you have that?" I eyed the gun warily. "Should I be sleeping with one eye open this year?"

Giggling, Trina picked the gun up. "Don't worry this isn't for you. It's for MagiX."

"MagiX?" I cocked my head to the side and then my eyes widened in recognition. "Oh, yeah. I remember now. Something kind of like the Olympics but for magical beings?"

Leaning the barrel of the gun against her shoulder, she struck a dramatic pose. "Well, not that big of a deal. I mean, it's mainly between the colleges in the U.S., and other countries have their own thing." She scratched the back of her head and laughed.

"I'm sure what we call the MagiX Games is not the same thing as the rest of the world."

I scooched closer, my lips pursed. "But it involves guns?"

"And potion balls!" She grinned a bit too proud of herself. "Now that I'm over nineteen, I can participate. You should think about signing up too."

I sat back on my bed and rubbed the side of my face, all the information too much for me to handle. "I'm still getting used to all this magic stuff, I'm not adding something like this to my stress. Also, I'm not competitive at all."

"Sure, you're not." She tossed the gun onto her bed and tried to force some of the clothes back into her bag. "Anyway, I only brought the essentials."

I giggled, moving away from my bed to pick up a pair of suspenders. "The essentials, huh? And what do your parents think of your rock star sister's influence on you?"

Trina snagged the suspenders from me with a wink. "They were about as happy as when I announced I liked girls," she shrugged a shoulder, "and then a bit happier when I said that I was going to use my new style to build my own little harem."

I rolled my eyes. "They're not my harem."

Snorting, Trina flopped on her bed. "You're dating all of them?"

"Yeah," I drew out, watching her carefully.

"And you're having sex with them?"

"Well, not all of them."

"But you will eventually? That's the plan, right?" Trina grinned mischievously.

I couldn't lie. I did plan on getting the full experience, and that included having sex with Aidan and Ian. Especially, Ian and that piercing. A small involuntary shudder went through me.

"What was that for?" Trina arched a brow.

I flushed. "Nothing."

"What nothing? You shivered." Trina went up onto one foot, a knee on the ground. "Was that a good shiver or a bad one? Do I need to lop someone's dick off? Because I can and will."

I laughed and waved her off. "Please don't! I still have plans for those dicks. Especially, the pierced one."

Trina stared at me for a second confusion fluttered across her face, then a light bulb went off in her big head of hair. A sly grin went up her face. "Which one has the Prince Albert?"

Laughing and dancing away from her, I pretended to unpack my bag again. "So, what classes do you have this year?"

"Oh, no, you don't. You can't drop that bombshell and then change the subject." Trina grabbed at me, but I darted away, jumping onto the bed.

"It's no big deal really."

"No big deal?" Trina climbed onto the bed, her hands out to stop me from running. "This guy is literally pierced, ribbed for your pleasure, and you think it's no big deal?"

"Okay, sort of a big deal." I shrugged. "But I haven't even had sex with him yet, so I wouldn't know if it were like that or not."

Trina stopped trying to block me, a pensive look on her face. "Okay, so that narrows it down. You haven't had sex with him yet." She tapped her chin and climbed off the bed. "It can't be Dale because your mom already told me about the incident at your house."

"Oh my god. She didn't." I rushed off the bed in a hurry. "Please tell me she's not going around telling everyone I'm having orgies because I already assured her that was not how it was happening."

"Good to know." Trina winked. "And no. Just that you don't respect the sanity of your parents. Really, Max. You need to up your silencing spells. Libby and I have done it all over campus, and you never hear about us getting caught."

My face heated. "I have plenty of respect for my parents' sanity. They don't have any for me. I've been scarred by them plenty of times. It's time I return the favor." I placed my hands on my hips and nodded, firmly.

Trina let out a puff of air. "Okay, whatever you say. Now back to the matter at hand." She grabbed a pair of boots with way too many spikes on the sides. One kick with those shoes? Ouch.

"Are you hungry?" I asked climbing off the bed. I grabbed my phone, shoving it into my back pocket. "I'm thinking of grabbing something to eat in the cafeteria."

"Or you could go off campus with one of your piercing-less boyfriends." Trina taunted, trying but failing to get me to relent.

I wagged my brows at her and pulled open the door. "Maybe."

"I'm your roommate. You are bound by roommate law to tell me all your dark and naughty secrets." She trailed after me with new-found energy.

"I don't remember reading any roommate laws." I rolled my eyes at her. "And I don't see you giving up all your dark and naughty secrets."

"That's because I don't have any," Trina pointed out. "I'm an open book. I date girls. I have too many siblings and not enough bathroom space, and I really really want to know who has the Prince Albert."

"Why?" I laughed. "You don't even like penis. Why so interested?"

"Now that's not true. I never said I didn't like penis, just that I like my sex with a little less penis," Trina rambled on.

"So, what, you're bi?" I arched a brow, not really caring what sex she prefers. I just enjoyed pushing her buttons.

Trina's eye brows scrunched together tightly. "Now, I'm not saying that either. I mean nothing against guys." She waved her hands at me as if I might attack her for insulting my boyfriends. "I just prefer mine soft and more..." she moved her hands in a cupping motion in front of her. "... round."

"You know there are guys with boobs, right? You can have boobs and all the penis you want." I snickered.

Opening her mouth to launch into what would probably be a debilitating argument about why she didn't want a penis, Trina finally caught the glint in my eye. "You're fucking with me, aren't you?"

I held my fingers up, pinching them together. "Just a bit."

"I'm going too far with the penis thing, aren't I?"

I grinned. "A bit."

We were quiet for a few moments before Trina just couldn't help herself.

"It's Ian?" Trina snapped, pointing a finger at me. I only gave her a coy grin, making her frown. "Or Aidan. It has to be Aidan. He's so big. A piercing wouldn't be that bad for a guy like him."

"If you say so," I taunted her, adding a skip to my step on my way to the cafeteria.

Trina chased after me, flipping back and forth between who she thought it was. "Oh, come on, I have to know."

"No, you don't." I quipped, spinning around in place which was why I didn't see Sabrina before I knocked her over and landed right on top of her.

"Ugh, get off." Sabrina pushed at me.

I climbed off her, offering her a hand. "Sorry."

Sabrina looked at my hand for a moment and then, to my surprise, took it. I pulled her to her feet and stood there awkwardly. "So, about Monica—"

"I don't want to talk about that traitor," Sabrina cut me off with a sneer.

My mouth fell open, taken back by the fierceness of her words. "Oh, okay."

Sabrina's face softened. "I mean, if she was hiding all that, who knows what else she could have done? I don't need someone like that hanging around me. I might be a bitch, but at least I'm upfront about it."

"Right?" The word came out slow and confused.

"What I mean to say is..." Sabrina sighed dramatically, crossing her arms over her chest. "Thank you."

"Thank you?"

"What, do I have an echo in here?" Sabrina rolled her eyes to the ceiling and then smiled at me. It wasn't one of her smirks or a I'm-pretending-to-like-you smile. Not even one of her fake smiles she saved for parents. This was a full-on genuine smile.

I was floored. I didn't know what to say to that, and apparently, I was staring for far longer than appropriate because Trina nudged me.

"Oh, uh. Yeah, you're welcome." I shook my head and smiled back. We both stood there for a moment not knowing what to do. I was more unsure with the blonde in front of me than all my boyfriends. How weird was that?

Trina, of course, had no problem breaking the ice. "So, Max was just telling me about how one of the guys has a Prince Albert, but she won't tell me which one."

Sabrina quirked a brow and then flipped her hair over her shoulder. "Oh, I totally know that one."

"Really?" Trina grinned and started toward the cafeteria once more. "Tell me. It's Aidan, isn't it."

I gaped at them as Trina grilled Sabrina Craftsman for information and the blonde let her.

"Are you coming or what?" Sabrina said over her shoulder.

"Uh, yeah." I hurried after them, my brain still not caught up to all that had just happened.

The coming out party after a few hiccups and one bad witch had turned out to be a blast. I'd made even more friends than before. I had four boyfriends. My parents liked said boyfriends. And now Sabrina was being nice to me. What was the world coming to?

Thank You for Reading!

Want to find out what happens to Max and her guys next?

Come hang out with me in my Reader's Group on Facebook!

Find out all about my works, sneak peeks of works in progress, and exclusive giveaways.

Don't want to interact but want to be on the up and up?

Follow me on Social Media
Facebook.com/erinrbedford
@erin_bedford

Want to be the first to know about my new releases?
Erinbedford.com/newsletter